PUFFIN B

There's a Viking in My B

Jeremy Strong once worked in a bakery, putting the jam into 3,000 doughnuts every night. Now he puts the jam in stories instead, which he finds much more exciting. At the age of three he fell out of a first-floor bedroom window and landed on his head. His mother says that this damaged him for the rest of his life and refuses to take any responsibility. He loves writing stories because he says it is 'the only time you alone have complete control and can make anything happen'. His ambition is to make you laugh (or at least snuffle). Jeremy Strong lives in Kent with his family and pets.

Jeremy Strong

There's a Viking in My Bed and Other Stories

Illustrated by John Levers

PUFFIN BOOKS

PUFFIN BOOKS

Published by the Penguin Group
Penguin Books Ltd, 80 Strand, London WC2R 0RL, England
Penguin Putnam Inc., 375 Hudson Street, New York, New York 10014, USA
Penguin Books Australia Ltd, Ringwood, Victoria, Australia
Penguin Books Canada Ltd, 10 Alcorn Avenue, Toronto, Ontario, Canada M4V 3B2
Penguin Books India (P) Ltd, 11 Community Centre, Panchsheel Park, New Delhi – 110 017, India
Penguin Books (NZ) Ltd, Cnr Rosedale and Airborne Roads, Albany, Auckland, New Zealand
Penguin Books (South Africa) (Pty) Ltd, 24 Sturdee Avenue, Rosebank 2196 South Africa

Penguin Books Ltd, Registered Offices: 80 Strand, London WC2R 0RL, England

www.penguin.com

There's a Viking in My Bed first published by A & C Black (Publishers) Ltd 1990
Published in Puffin Books 1992
Viking in Trouble first published by A & C Black (Publishers) Ltd 1992
Published in Puffin Books 1995
Viking at School first published by A & C Black (Publishers) Ltd 1997
Published in Puffin Books 1998

This edition published in Puffin Books 2001
3

Puffin Film and TV Tie-in edition first published 2001

Text copyright © Jeremy Strong, 1990, 1992, 1997
Illustrations copyright © John Levers, 1990, 1992, 1997
All rights reserved

The moral right of the author has been asserted

Made and printed in England by Clays Ltd, St Ives plc

British Library Cataloguing in Publication Data
A CIP catalogue record for this book is available from the British Library

ISBN 0–141–31025–1

Contents

There's a Viking in My Bed   1

Viking in Trouble   65

Viking at School   129

There's a Viking in My Bed

For Zoe and Tim – who else!

Crash Landing

Through the mist came the creak of many oars. Now and then there was a splash. The grey mist swirled and slid over the flat, grey sea, but not a sign could be seen of the boats: only the steady slap of oars and a few low curses.

Then a dark shadow moved within the mist, growing blacker as it came nearer, until the great wooden hulk of a Viking war-boat emerged, trailing wisps of fog along its sides. Twenty oars bit into the water, and forty Viking warriors strained over the heavy poles.

'Never have I seen a fog like this,' hissed the leader. He was a tall Dane, with a huge moustache and beard, fiery red. 'There is something I do not like about it.' He cast a glance at the lookout, standing up by the great dragon-head prow. 'Is there no sign of the fleet? Where are the other boats?'

The lookout sucked one finger and held it up, as if to judge the wind direction. He stared into the mist, took off his helmet and pulled out both ears like radar scanners. His ears were big and red. The Viking leader cursed.

'Sigurd is an idiot. Why do we use a fool for a lookout?' Beside him, Tostig laughed. 'It's quite simple, Ulric. Sigurd can't row or cook. What else is there for him to do? You know what happened the last time he was at the oars. We ended up going round in a circle for almost an hour. And when he was cook, he boiled up all our best meat in a pot of seawater – urgh! At least he's safe up there.'

Ulric Blacktooth spat. 'Look at him, holding out his ears. What a fool!' He shouted forward. 'What can you see, Sigurd?'

'There's a lot of mist about,' answered the lookout. 'No, no, wait, there's something else. I can see something else through the mist!'

Ulric Blacktooth gripped the mast. Had they found the rest of the war-party at last? 'What is it? What can you see?'

'Wait a minute, the mist is clearing. Yes! I can see it quite clearly now.'

'What is it, what is it?' bellowed Ulric impatiently.

'There's water below, Ulric. I can see water. It's – the sea!'

Ulric Blacktooth shut his eyes and banged his head several times against the ship's mast. 'Tostig,' he hissed, 'that man will be the death of us all. Why are we cursed with such a fool?'

Tostig was snorting through his nose, a sure sign that he was losing his temper. Temper-losing was something that Tostig was very good at. He did it quite often – and practice makes perfect.

Now he drew his sword, which he had named
Heartsplitter, and strode forward. In a moment he
was beside the lookout.

'Sigurd, of course you can see the sea. We are on
a boat. We are *at* sea.' Tostig spoke as if he wanted
each word to hit Sigurd like a hammer. 'Now,
Sigurd, if you wish to stay alive, *do something useful!*
Get yourself up that dragon's head, sit on top and don't
say a word until you see the English coast. Do you hear?'

So saying, Tostig thrust his sword (the pointed
end) very close to Sigurd's backside. Sigurd gave a
jump and scuttled up the prow, until he was right
on the dragon's head. From there he turned and
looked back at Tostig. 'I was only trying to help,'
he complained.

Tostig grunted and returned to Ulric, while Sigurd sighed and tried very hard to see through all the mist that surrounded them. He was bored and tired. He had been on lookout duty for days. For some strange reason, nobody would let him row. Sigurd had always thought rowing was his best subject.

The boat was part of a large Viking raiding fleet, headed for England. They had been at sea for seven days, and the mist had been with them for the last twenty-four hours. It was a creepy, evil mist, making everyone nervous and jumpy. Somehow they had become separated from the rest of the fleet. Now they were drifting, they knew not where.

Sigurd strained his eyes to see through the swirling greyness. He pricked up his ears. What was that? Could he hear something? There was the splashing of the oars, but was there something else, perhaps the sound of breakers? Sigurd perched as far forward as possible, lying across the dragon's nose. He thought of shouting to Ulric and Tostig, but they'd only be cross.

Sigurd stared and stared. The mist seemed even thicker. But the noise was louder now. It *was* breakers, surely? That could only mean one thing. They were close to land – maybe too close. Breakers meant a coastline, and that could mean rocks. He must tell Ulric. They were close to land at last.

'Ulric! Tostig! There's . . .'

At that same moment there was a sickening crunch and the longship ran headlong on to low rocks. Sigurd was catapulted into the clammy English sea. The boat shuddered and stopped. Ulric picked himself up from the deck and shouted to the men.

'Reverse, quick, hard astern, go back, turn about! Full speed backwards!'

Twenty oars plunged into the sea, and the Vikings strained every muscle to move their boat off the rocks. Slowly the great wooden keel slid back. Slowly the sea caught hold of the longship and pulled her clear.

'Back, back!' Ulric bellowed, as the warboat gained speed. 'Where's that idiot of a lookout?'

Tostig glanced at the dragon's head. 'Sorry to report, Ulric, I think he went overboard when we hit the rocks.'

Ulric was about to shout, 'Man overboard!', but stopped himself just in time. Sigurd overboard? What a relief! Ulric smiled. 'Full speed ahead, muffled oars,' he commanded, and the longship slid silently away into the misty North Sea.

Sigurd was not happy. The English sea was wet and cold. This was something he had always suspected, and he was disappointed to find it true. Why hadn't they gone to the South of France for a raid? The sea was warm and blue there. Why did they have to come to grotty old Britain? He pulled a large piece of seaweed from beneath his helmet and waded ashore.

Sigurd stood on the beach. Cold salt water ran out of his helmet and down his spine. It trickled down his legs and filled his boots. It was not a nice feeling. He walked forward a few steps, slipped on a dead jellyfish and fell flat on his back in a rock pool. A large crab took an angry swipe at one of his big red ears, then marched away.

'Ow!' Sigurd scrambled to his feet. 'This isn't my lucky day,' he muttered. 'Well, there is only one thing to do. If the others are not here to raid a village, I shall just have to raid one by myself.' He drew his trusty (and rusty) sword, which he had named Nosepicker, and set off across the beach.

It did not take long to find the path up the cliffs. Indeed, Sigurd was surprised to find good steps cut into the rock face. He moved with all the stealth of a Viking raider, or so he thought. Here came the great warrior, eyes ablaze, sword drawn, soggy feet squelching in sodden boots!

The mist did not make things easier. It still clung to almost everything, and there was little that Sigurd could see. At last he reached the top of the cliffs and he followed the well-worn path ahead. He felt there were buildings near-by before he actually saw them. The path became hard beneath his feet. It was made of something he had never seen before. Sigurd's heart beat faster.

A cat ran yowling across his feet. Sigurd took a swipe with Nosepicker and almost chopped off his toes. Now he really could see houses. They were huge – much larger than he had expected. They had hard walls, and in the window spaces there was something he had never seen before. It was dark and shiny.

Sigurd peered more closely and suddenly saw a fierce warrior glaring back at him. 'Yargh!' yelled Sigurd and thrust forward with Nosepicker. There was a shattering sound and the enemy had gone. Sigurd leaped backwards. What kind of magic was this?

The mist was clearing all the time and Sigurd began to see such strange things. He could not even begin to describe them: there were no words in his language to do so. Things with wheels – yes, round wheels, but such small wheels, and certainly not made of wood. They were thick and black and had peculiar-shaped things on top.

Suddenly, two bright eyes appeared. Huge white eyes, glaring at him from the mist. There was a strange clinking sound. The eyes started forward. They stopped. They started again, and were getting closer and closer. Sigurd drew back into the darkness of a doorway. His shoulder pressed against something small and round.

'Bing-bong, bing-bong, bing-bong.' Every time he moved, the same weird sound went off in his left ear.

The bright eyes came closer still. A misty shape moved behind them, carrying something that clinked. The eyes whirred and moved away. Sigurd began to breathe more easily.

'Bing-bong, bing-bong.'

The door behind him began to open. Sigurd sprang to life and was off like a hare. He ran and ran, wherever the hard concrete paths took him. At one moment he saw those bright eyes again. They were moving much faster, coming straight at him and roaring angrily. Sigurd threw himself down a side path and one of those odd shapes on wheels rushed by. Sigurd stood there panting. He must find somewhere safe to hide.

He staggered up the path, his heart pounding. Then all at once he stopped. Right in front of him was a big picture: a portrait of himself! There were the moustache and beard. There were the horned helmet and handsome nose. There was Nosepicker, held aloft. It was himself, no question.

Sigurd the Viking smiled and nodded. There was some strange lettering underneath which did not make sense, but Sigurd didn't care. Surely this was his home? He would be safe here at the sign of The Viking. He grinned up at the picture, mounted the steps, opened the door and went inside.

Outside, the Viking on the sign almost appeared to wink. The writing underneath said:

THE VIKING HOTEL
Every modern comfort
MANAGERS: MR AND MRS ELLIS
Rooms available now

2

Double Booking

By eight o'clock in the morning, the mist had quite cleared and few people even realised it had been there earlier. The summer sun was now warming the pavements, and the sign outside The Viking Hotel swung a little on squeaky hinges. The Viking warrior did not seem quite so splendid in full sunlight. It was easy to see that the paint was peeling in many places. In fact, the warrior looked rather the worse for wear, as did the rest of The Viking Hotel.

Paint was flaking from the window frames. Plants were wilting in the flower troughs. Dust and litter had blown up against the corners of the walls and stayed there.

Mr Ellis fetched a broom and sighed. It was the same every day. He didn't know where the dirt came from, but it kept coming. He had washed the front windows only two days ago, and already they were smeary. It was no wonder there were hardly any guests at the hotel. It was the height of the summer season: the place should be full to bursting, but out of twelve guest rooms, only three were booked.

Mr Ellis swept the front steps clean and went back inside.

'Are you children up yet?' he called up the stairs. There was a distant reply of thumping feet. He went to help his wife get breakfast ready and lay the tables in the dining room.

Suddenly the staircase was filled with thunder. It shook and rattled as if an entire North American buffalo herd had decided to migrate down it. Zoe and Tim appeared breathless at the kitchen door.

'What's the matter, Mum?' Zoe asked, wondering why her mother was standing so still and pale. Mrs Ellis blinked.

'Oh, nothing. I just thought someone had fallen down the stairs. For a moment, just for a moment, I was seriously worried. I might have known it was you two getting up.'

'What's for brekkers?' asked Tim, grabbing a banana from one of the plates.

'Put it back. That's for the Ambrose boy, and you know how fussy he is. I don't know why his parents let him get away with it. You can have breakfast when you've laid the tables.'

Their father pointed to the dining room. 'Don't forget the small glasses for fruit juice.'

It did not take long to set the tables, with so few guests. As soon as they were finished, Zoe and Tim went back to the kitchen, where Mr Ellis was frying some eggs for them. He asked them what they were planning to do all day. Zoe looked across at Tim and shrugged.

'There is some shopping that needs doing,' suggested Mrs Ellis. 'Don't forget we have a new guest arriving this morning – Mrs Tibblethwaite.'

'Mrs what?' squeaked Tim.

'Tibblethwaite.'

'Fiddleplate?' Tim repeated, his small tongue struggling to go in three different directions at once.

'Oh, dear,' smiled Mrs Ellis, 'you'd better get it right before she arrives. Try again – Tibblethwaite.'

'Mrs Tiddlefate!' Tim jumped up with delight. 'There! I've got it, I've got it – Mrs Piddlegate!'

'Oh, Tim,' sighed Zoe. 'Come on, let's go and get the shopping.'

Mrs Ellis gave her daughter a list and asked her to see if she could get some sense into Tim before the new guest arrived. Mr Ellis watched them set off and then turned to his wife.

'I don't suppose he'll get it right. He's only five and it *is* a difficult name. Perhaps Mrs Tibblethwaite won't mind. Just think, we'll have four rooms booked!'

'Is her room ready?' asked Mrs Ellis.

'I did it last night. Honestly Penny, I don't know what we're going to do. We'll be completely broke soon. Nobody comes because the place looks like a dump, so we never make enough money to do it up again. It's a trap.'

Penny Ellis slipped her arms round her husband's waist and hugged him. 'Don't worry. Something will turn up.'

'You're right. Something has turned up – Mrs Tibblethwaite. And she's early. You finish off the breakfasts. I'll see to her.'

The latest guest was standing on the front step, looking at the hotel sign with some suspicion. She was a short, rather heavily built lady, with a large hat and even larger suitcase.

'Good morning,' cried Mr Ellis, flashing his best smile. 'You must be Mrs Tibblethwaite. You've arrived early.'

'Good morning,' replied the lady stonily. 'I always arrive early. You must be The Viking Hotel.'

'I'm Mr Ellis. Did you have a good journey?'

'No. The train was late: somebody smoked in a no-smoking compartment so I pulled the alarm cord. The train stopped and I was fined fifty pounds because they said it wasn't an emergency. I told them it most certainly *was* an emergency if I was going to be forced to die of lung cancer. And then the taxi couldn't find this place at all.'

'I expect the driver took you to the Viking Cafe,' said Mr Ellis. 'They often make that mistake.' But Mrs Tibblethwaite was hardly paying any attention to him.

'We went to The Viking Cafe, The Viking Restaurant, The Viking's Delight, The Viking Chinese Take-away and The Viking Burgerbar.'

'Well, you're here now,' smiled Mr Ellis, seizing the heavy suitcase. 'Follow me, and I'll show you to your room.'

'Just why are there so many Viking places around here?' asked Mrs Tibblethwaite, stomping up the stairs behind Mr Ellis.

'Ah, well, over a thousand years ago, Flotby was a favourite target for the Viking raiders from Denmark. There are lots of Viking relics round here and we have a Viking Festival at the end of every summer. Now, the bathroom is at the end of the corridor. You've got a lovely view of the sea from Room Four. The other guests are at breakfast now. Would you like to join them?'

'No thank you, I ate on the train. I don't know what it was. It arrived on a plate all wrapped up: I suppose they were afraid it might spread germs if it wasn't kept wrapped. Anyhow, I'm not hungry. What time is lunch?'

'That's at one o'clock. You'll see all the hotel details on the notice in your room.' Mr Ellis opened the door to Room Four and pushed the suitcase in.

Then he hurried back downstairs to help with the breakfasts.

'What's she like?' asked Mrs Ellis under her breath, as they passed between the tables pouring coffee and serving extra toast.

'She'll eat you for dinner. One gulp and you'll be gone.'

'Oh dear, all I need now is a difficult guest – as if the Ambroses aren't bad enough.'

At that moment, there was a loud cry from the top of the stairs.

'Mr Ellis! Mr Ellis! I say, Mr Ellis!'

Penny grinned at her husband. 'Oh Mr Ellis, I think that's your favourite guest, Mr Ellis. Do go and see what the matter is!'

'I'll give you "Mr Ellis",' he growled. He put down the coffee pot and hurried to the staircase.

'Mr Ellis,' cried Mrs Tibblethwaite, clutching the stair rail with one hand. Her face was white and trembling.

Mr Ellis took the stairs two at a time. 'Whatever is the matter?'

'Mr Ellis, there's a Viking in my bed!'

'What on earth do you mean?'

Mrs Tibblethwaite suddenly stopped shaking, drew herself up to her full (small) height and fixed Mr Ellis with two extraordinarily dagger-like eyes. 'I mean, Mr Ellis, that there is a Viking in my bed. What do you think I mean? If I say there is a

Viking in my bed, I *mean* there is a Viking in my bed. Why don't you come and look for yourself?'

She grabbed Mr Ellis by one arm and hauled him off down the corridor. She kicked open her bedroom door and pushed Mr Ellis in front of her. He entered the room carefully and went across to the bed. No. There was nothing. Certainly the covers were all mucked up as if someone had slept there, but there was no sign of a soul.

'I think you must have been dreaming, Mrs Tibblethwaite.'

'I was not dreaming, Mr Ellis. There was a Viking in my bed. Good heavens man, do you think I don't know a Viking when I see one? He still had his helmet on. And his boots! I insist that you search the room.'

Mr Ellis groaned. He got down on his hands and knees and looked beneath the bed. He pulled back the curtains and shouted, 'Boo!'

'There's no need to act the fool,' said Mrs Tibblethwaite coldly.

'There's nobody here,' said Mr Ellis, crossing to the wardrobe and pulling open the double doors.

A million coathangers seemed to burst from the wardrobe and a monster sprang yelling into the room, all arms and legs and hair. His black tangled beard had bits of seaweed hanging from it. His eyes glittered from beneath huge, shaggy eyebrows and a dented, two-horned helmet.

Sigurd snatched Nosepicker from the scabbard, glaring at the two strange creatures in front of him.

'Raargh!' he snarled, swishing Nosepicker through the air and slicing off a bit of curtain. 'Rrraargh!'

Mr Ellis simply stared, quite stupified. His brain had gone into shock. He could not move his tongue or lips. No sound would come from his throat. His feet felt as if they had been nailed to the floor. His arms were like lead sausage rolls.

Mrs Tibblethwaite poked him. 'There, you see? I told you there was a Viking in my bed. Now, if this is some kind of welcome committee, I don't think very much of it. And if it's some kind of joke, it isn't very funny. Don't just stand there, Mr Ellis, do something.'

Mr Ellis did do something. He fainted. Sigurd gave a loud laugh and stepped towards Mrs Tibblethwaite.

'Oh no, you don't, you overgrown hairpiece. Take that, and that!' She began to beat the Viking with her handbag, almost knocking his helmet off.

Sigurd yelped, decided he'd had enough and ran from the room. He plunged down the stairs and almost fell headlong into the dining room, stopping himself just in time. He stood on the bottom step, panting and brandishing Nosepicker, while seven very startled hotel guests put down their toast and coffee and stared back at him.

3

Discoveries

Tim and Zoe walked into the dining room to discover their mother and seven guests huddled together on one side, while a strange hairy man glared at them from the other.

'Hello,' shouted Tim. 'Who are you? I like your sword.'

Before Mrs Ellis could make a grab at him, Tim was walking across the room, a big smile on his face. 'Is it a real sword or just plastic? I bet it's plastic.'

Sigurd watched Tim warily, but the boy was only a small child. He couldn't do any harm to a fierce Viking warrior like himself. Sigurd grinned back: he was a nice-looking lad.

'It is plastic, isn't it?' laughed Tim. 'That's why you're smiling. Come on, show me.' With that, he calmly reached out and took the sword from Sigurd.

It was difficult to tell who was the most surprised. Sigurd was left empty-handed and un-armed. A five-year-old child had just taken his sword from him. Was he dreaming? No, because Tim had collapsed to the floor beneath the weight of the weapon. His eyes were popping.

'Wow! It *is* a real sword. A real, real, really real sword! Hey Zoe, it's a real sword!'

At that moment, Mr Ellis appeared at the top of the stairs with Mrs Tibblethwaite. Poor Mr Ellis was still in a state of shock. This was not surprising, because Mrs Tibblethwaite had spent the last three minutes trying to bring him round from his faint. First of all she had sat him upright and slapped his face several times. His cheeks were still red and sore. That hadn't worked so she'd begun to give him the kiss of life. At this point, Mr Ellis had woken up, found himself being kissed to death by Mrs Tibblethwaite and promptly fainted again, so the stout lady had jabbed him with her hat pin. That soon had him on his feet.

Now the pair were coming slowly downstairs, while Sigurd looked about in desperation. He was surrounded. He could not imagine where he was. This was a nightmare. None of the great stories of raids he had heard in Denmark had prepared him for anything like this. He had never before seen a room or people like these. Truly, this was some horrible nightmare he was in.

Sweat broke out on his forehead. The voices around him seemed to swim through his brain, echoing and gurgling. The walls of the dining room grew taller and taller until they started to bend in towards him, falling on him, falling ...

Sigurd tottered forward and crashed uncon-scious across a breakfast table.

A glass of orange juice flew through the air, nicely sprinkling the guests as it passed overhead. A plate of egg and bacon spun off the table like some weird flying saucer. It deposited its pass-engers in an eggy mess on the carpet, then flew on, hit a wall and shattered.

Sigurd lay across the table, quite still. There was a short silence and then everyone started shouting and screaming at once. Mrs Ellis rushed across and hugged Tim, although he hadn't got a clue why. Mr Ellis ran down the stairs calling for calm.

'It's quite all right, everyone. Sorry about the unexpected guest. He's obviously some party-goer

who had too much to drink last night. If you wouldn't mind going to the lounge, we'll clear up and serve breakfast again in ten minutes. I do apologise for this most unexpected event.'

Mrs Ellis helped some of the guests out of the room, while Mrs Tibblethwaite stood at the top of the stairs, watching with one raised eyebrow. 'Do I understand, Mr Ellis, that you don't know this creature?'

'Of course not, Mrs Tibblethwaite.' Mr Ellis groaned as he tried to move Sigurd's heavy body from the table. His foot caught on a chair leg and the two of them crashed to the floor.

'Oh, for goodness sake!' cried the stout lady, marching down the stairs. 'Let me give you a hand.'

'Are you all right, Dad?' asked Zoe. There was a muffled reply and Mr Ellis crawled out from beneath the Viking. Together they turned Sigurd over so that he was facing the ceiling.

'What a mess. Look at him, drunk as a pig,' snapped Mrs Tibblethwaite.

'It's a brill sword, Dad,' cried Tim. 'Look!'

'It's a pretty good costume too,' Zoe added. 'It's so real. Pongs a bit, though.'

Mrs Tibblethwaite sniffed loudly. 'That's the drink.'

'I don't think so,' murmured Mr Ellis. 'Smells more like sea-water to me – and old food and damp leather.'

'Disgusting. He should be put in a bath at once.'

Mr Ellis thought for a moment. Penny asked if she should call the police, but her husband shook his head. 'This man is only drunk. I bet he'll have a splitting headache – and feel very embarrassed – when he wakes up. We'll put him in Room Twelve, where he can sleep it off. Mrs Tibblethwaite, would you mind helping us get this Viking up to Room Twelve? I'm so sorry you found him in your bedroom. I can't think how it happened.'

Surprisingly, Mrs Tibblethwaite was now quite calm about the whole business. 'It's all right, Mr Ellis. Hotel rooms are usually such dull places. I must admit it was a shock to find him asleep in my bed, but at least it's something I shall remember for a long time. I'll take his left leg.'

It took five of them to carry Sigurd up the stairs to Room Twelve, and there they laid him out on the bed.

'Well,' said Mrs Tibblethwaite, 'all that excitement has made me hungry. Perhaps I'll have breakfast after all.'

'Of course. The other guests will want some too.' Mrs Ellis hurried back downstairs.

'I'm just coming,' added her husband. 'Tim, Zoe, stay here and keep an eye on this chap, will you? Come and tell us the moment he wakes up.'

Downstairs, The Viking Hotel returned to normal. All was calm in the dining room as the guests finally finished their breakfast, and soon the unwelcome visitor was forgotten.

However, things in Room Twelve were not calm at all. Just as Tim and Zoe were beginning to get rather bored with watching a sleeping body, Sigurd began to stir. He opened his eyes and tried to sit up. Then he clutched his head and fell back.

'He's got a headache,' said Zoe. 'Dad said he'd have a headache. Give him some water, Timmy.'

Sigurd took the water gratefully, and managed to prop himself up on a few pillows while he drank. He glanced at the two children and round the room. He felt for his sword, but of course it was gone.

Sigurd sighed. It was quite plain to him that he had been captured. Now he would probably be killed. There was no mercy for Viking raiders.

'Hello,' smiled Zoe. 'I'm Zoe. This is my brother, Timmy.'

'Tim, not Timmy,' grunted her brother.

'How do you feel?' said Zoe.

Sigurd listened to the strange noises being made by the children. He could not understand a word. Zoe was watching his face carefully. 'I don't think he understands, Tim. I don't think he's English.'

'Of course he isn't. He's a Viking, a real Viking.'

'Don't be stupid.' Zoe pointed at herself and said her name several times. Sigurd nodded. He pointed at himself, too, and repeated, 'Zoe, Zoe.'

'No, not you, *me*!' She took the Viking's hand and used it to point at herself. 'Zoe,' she said once more. Then she made Sigurd point at Tim and she said his name, too.

Sigurd's face lit up with a grin. 'Ah, Zoe!' he cried. Then he pointed at her brother. 'Timmy!'

'Not Timmy! Tim!'

The Viking pointed at himself. 'Sigurd,' he announced proudly.

Tim glanced up at the big warrior. 'Well, I'm going to call him Siggy,' he said moodily. The Viking banged his chest and glared back at Tim.

'Sigurd,' he repeated. 'Hedeby. Sigurd, Hedeby.'

'All right,' muttered Tim. 'Keep your hair on. If you want to be called Sigurd Hedeby, you can call me Tim Ellis. In fact, you can call me Master Tim Ellis.'

'Oh do shut up, Tim,' Zoe butted in, giving her brother a push. 'You do go on sometimes. Didn't he say Hedeby?'

'Sigurd, Hedeby,' nodded the Viking, and he started pointing all over again. 'Zoe, Tim, Sigurd, Hedeby.'

'*Master* Tim Ellis!' insisted Tim. 'Will you stop pushing me, Zoe!'

'You don't understand, do you, Tim? Sigurd keeps saying Hedeby, but it's not part of his name. I think it's where he comes from.'

'What do you mean?'

Zoe shook her head. Her face was pale and excited. 'We learned about Hedeby at school. It was a famous Viking settlement in Denmark.'

'But he is a Viking,' said Tim. 'So what's so special about that?'

'Hedeby doesn't exist any more. It was a Viking town, hundreds of years ago. It's not there any more, but here's Sigurd, and he says he comes from Hedeby!'

Tim groaned. 'Well of course he does. A real Viking wouldn't come from anywhere else, would he? I told you he was a real Viking!'

4

Lunch – Viking Style

Tim and Zoe's parents were reluctant to listen to their story of the real Viking in Room Twelve, let alone believe it. The children had to wait until all the breakfast things had been cleared away, and the washing-up done. Then Zoe dragged her parents up the two flights of stairs to Room Twelve, where Tim was busily trying on Sigurd's helmet.

The Viking was very worried when Mr and Mrs Ellis appeared. He still thought he was due for execution. But Zoe reassured him by introducing everyone. Her father felt rather foolish saying, 'Good morning, Sigurd,' and shaking hands with a Viking. But Sigurd was proud of his own party piece: 'Sigurd, Hedeby, Denmark.'

Mrs Ellis shook her head. 'He's just pretending. He must be English. He doesn't want us to know who he is so he can't be charged for all the damage he's caused.'

Zoe had fetched some drawing paper and pencils. She sat down on the edge of the bed and sketched the whole Ellis family, writing their names underneath.

'Hey, that's not me,' Tim complained. 'I'm not fat.' Zoe ignored him, and all the time she drew, she told Sigurd what she was doing. 'This is me, this is my dad, Mr Ellis . . .' And so she went on. She drew the hotel and the sign. Sigurd pointed to it excitedly. Finally Zoe stopped and gave him the pencil.

He stared at the thin piece of wood as if it was something magical. It was quite plain that he had never seen a pencil in his whole life. Zoe looked up at her parents. 'See?' she said.

'He's kidding us,' muttered her father.

Siggy now began to make a few practice strokes with the pencil, then slowly and carefully he started to draw. The others crowded round the bed. A tense, fascinated silence descended on them. Siggy's story slowly took shape on the paper. He drew his house and the longships, including an ugly and fierce-looking warrior with a vast beard. (This was Ulric Blacktooth and it was a good thing that Ulric wasn't around to see it.) He drew the ships setting sail, the mist and how he'd fallen into the sea.

'Now do you believe us?' Zoe asked in a whisper, as Sigurd put down the pencil and looked at them all in turn.

Mrs Ellis hesitated. 'I really don't know, dear. I mean, you must admit, it doesn't seem all that possible.'

Her husband grunted. 'I'm fed up with this play-acting. This man is no more a Viking than I am. He's just some left-over drunk from a fancy dress party.' He turned to Sigurd and felt his rough leather jacket. 'I bet you he's got his driving licence on him somewhere – and all his credit cards. That will prove who he is.'

Tim giggled. 'Vikings don't have driving licences!'

'He's not a Viking!' shouted Mr Ellis, standing up. 'I'm going to ring the police. He's bound to have been reported missing.'

But nothing of the kind had happened. Two very polite policemen came to the hotel. They asked Sigurd several questions, which of course he didn't understand. They searched his clothes and found nothing but a few seashells and a small dead crab. They told Mr Ellis that, as far as the police were concerned, there was little they could do. Then they left.

'Does this mean we can keep him, Daddy?' asked Zoe.

'Zoe! We're not talking about some pet animal. Sigurd is a human being – I think. I suppose he'll have to stay here until we find out more about him.'

'Another mouth to feed,' Mrs Ellis complained.

'Yes. Well, he'll just have to work for his living. He can help in the kitchen with the washing-up.'

'I suppose he's probably hungry now,' said Mrs Ellis. 'We'd better take him down for lunch. He can sit in the corner of the dining room.'

'Are you hungry?' Tim asked brightly. Sigurd frowned. 'Oh, you know, Siggy. Food, nosh, lovely grub – din-dins.' Tim's father rolled his eyes at the level of this intelligent conversation. Siggy still didn't understand, not until Zoe pretended she was eating. Then his eyes lit up and he banged his stomach with both fists. He made a sweeping circle with his hands, as if to show that he had an enormous appetite.

'That's what I was afraid of,' said Mrs Ellis, as they went downstairs.

The Viking had not eaten for more than twenty-four hours, and he glared at the other guests in the dining room as if he would have liked to swallow *them*. The Ambrose family were so put off that they hid behind their menu cards, whilst their charming son, Roger, did a few experiments to see how long it took to empty the salt cellar into the water jug.

Siggy stared at the clean white tablecloths and napkins, the placemats and cutlery. Most odd, he thought. He picked up a table knife, ran his thumb down the blade and threw it to the floor. What a useless knife! You couldn't kill a grasshopper with something as puny as that.

Zoe brought in some roast chicken and put it on the table. As she turned her back to fetch the vegetables and gravy, Sigurd seized a chicken leg and ate it in three seconds flat. He tore the meat off with his teeth and threw the bone over his shoulder. It disappeared half-way up the stairs, bounced off the banisters and hit Roger on the back of the head.

'Ow! I wasn't doing nothing!' muttered Roger, thinking his father had just clipped him round the ear.

When Zoe returned with the gravy, Siggy took the gravy boat and began to drink straight from it, mistaking it for beer. He took two huge swigs. His eyes almost exploded, his cheeks swelled up and he spat the whole lot out over the tablecloth.

'Siggy!' Zoe cried. 'What on earth did you do that for?'

'Urgh, urgh,' said Sigurd, drawing his sleeve across his mouth.

The other guests watched with horror. Mrs Ambrose bent over her son and whispered in his ear. 'Don't think you can behave like that, Roger. The man's a monster.'

Zoe tried to put some Brussels sprouts and carrots on Sigurd's plate, but he swept the whole lot to the floor. He wanted meat – and lots of it. He pushed back his chair and went to all the other tables, seizing any chicken that was left and cramming it into his mouth.

'Hey,' cried Mr Ambrose. 'That's my chicken!' He tried to grab Sigurd's arm, but the Viking growled and fixed him with such a fierce stare that he meekly put his hands in his lap.

'You're a coward, Herbert Ambrose,' hissed his wife. 'You've got to stand up to him. Ask him for your chicken back!'

'But he's eaten it!'

'Huh, any excuse! You're just a wimp. I always knew you were a wimp. You were a wimp when I married you and you're still a wimp.'

Poor Mr Ambrose was bright red and slowly turning purple. 'If I'm a wimp then you're a...you're a squidface!' he blurted out – and seeing the look of shocked surprise on his wife's face, he went on. 'You were a squidface when I married you and you're still a squidface.'

Now he was laughing hysterically. His wife picked up her fork and jabbed at him.

Zoe had already rushed back to the kitchen to fetch help, and her parents came hurrying into the dining room to sort things out. Siggy had just swiped the last of the chicken from the guests. The floor was littered with bones. Mr Ambrose was standing on a chair, shouting 'Squidface!' at the top of his voice; his wife was bombarding him with sprouts and carrots; Roger was hiding beneath the table, drinking boatfuls of gravy and seeing how far he could spurt them out again.

Surprisingly, it was Mrs Tibblethwaite who came to the rescue. All this time she had been sitting in the far corner of the room, sternly watching everything. Now she rose to her feet and pushed back her chair.

'This has gone on quite long enough,' she announced. 'You ought to be ashamed of yourselves.' She marched across to Sigurd, grabbed him by the beard and led him back to his seat. Then she crossed to Mr Ambrose, yanked him from the chair and slapped his face, twice, pushing him into his place. She also slapped Mrs Ambrose across one cheek. Finally she reached under the table, hauled Roger out by the ear, gave it a good tweak and sat him down, too.

This was followed by a shocked silence, during which four people clutched their faces and watched Mrs Tibblethwaite warily. She glared back at them, breathing heavily, hands on her hips.

'I have never seen such behaviour at a dinner table in my life! Anyone would think this place was a zoo. Look at the state of this room. It must be cleared up at once, and you – all of you – are going to clean it!'

Mrs Ambrose choked. 'He started it,' she blurted out, pointing at Sigurd.

'That man is a Viking warrior,' said Mrs Tibblethwaite. 'How else do you expect him to behave? He doesn't know any better – but you do. Now start cleaning. Tim, fetch me Sigurd's sword!'

Tim ran from the room and quickly returned with the mighty weapon. Mrs Tibblethwaite took it and stood over the Ambroses as they got to work with mop and bucket.

'As soon as this is done, we're leaving!' hissed Mr Ambrose. 'This is the worst hotel we've ever stayed in. It's chaos and we're treated like slaves.'

'Just work and don't backchat,' warned Mrs Tibblethwaite, prodding him with Nosepicker.

Mr and Mrs Ellis had slumped into chairs in the kitchen.

'What are we going to do? That's three paying guests gone and one extra guest who squirts gravy everywhere. Oh Keith, we shall be ruined. We'll never have enough money to put things right!'

Her husband's face was stony. It was all too true. The kitchen door swung open and Mrs Tibblethwaite strode in.

'And what do you think you're doing, moping in here? Haven't you got a hotel to run? Come on, get on with it. People are still waiting for their lunch out there, and I don't suppose Sigurd has finished eating yet. You get some sausages cooking, while I sort out more vegetables. Come on, get cracking!'

5

Great Changes

The next few days seemed to pass in a haze. So many things happened that the Ellises could hardly keep pace. First of all they had to cope with Mrs Tibblethwaite and Sigurd. It was impossible to say which one was worse. Mrs Tibblethwaite seemed to have changed from being a guest to becoming one of the hotel managers. She was everywhere – ordering people about, cleaning, polishing and cooking. And although she got on everyone's nerves, it had to be admitted that she was a great help. Mr and Mrs Ellis would probably have given up if it hadn't been for her.

Siggy was like a giant, hairy child. His first ride in the car was remembered by most of Flotby. This was probably because he was so excited that he climbed out of the window and stood on the roof, waving Nosepicker and shouting to everyone, 'Good morning, how do you do?' (Zoe had taught him those words only the previous day, and he was still practising.)

Then there was the Viking's first bath. Zoe tried very hard to explain what he was meant to do. She ran a nice big hot bath. She showed him the soaps and shampoo. She acted out what bathing was all about. Then she pushed Siggy into the bathroom and shut the door. A few minutes later, she heard splashing and singing, and she happily went downstairs to report that all was well.

Five minutes passed, and Siggy appeared in the lounge. He was dripping wet, but still had all his clothes on: he'd smeared them with soap and shampoo. Shiny, multicoloured bubbles slowly slid down his chest and legs and popped from his armpits. For some strange reason he'd stuck a bar of soap on to each helmet horn.

'I don't think he understood me properly, Mum,' Zoe murmured.

Most spectacular of all was Sigurd's first attempt at helping out in the hotel. Mr and Mrs Ellis made him follow them round for a whole day, showing him what they had to do. He watched them vacuum. He picked up the pipe and put it to his face, only to have his beard sucked down it. Sigurd roared and ran off, dragging the vacuum cleaner behind him, until the plug was wrenched from the socket; the machine then stopped and the pipe released his beard.

Sigurd watched all the dirty sheets and towels go into the washing machine. He sat amazed while they spun round and round. He examined them carefully when they came out and flashed a broad smile at Zoe.

'Clean!' he said, and nodded with delight.

'He's learning ever so fast, Dad,' said Zoe.

'Good, he can do the washing up, then,' said Mr Ellis snappily – for this was the job he hated most of all. Besides, he was in a bad mood, still brooding on the problems of running a hotel with hardly any guests and a lot of bills to be paid.

The dirty dishes were piled up by the kitchen sink. Mr Ellis pointed at them. 'Sigurd, you clean? Understand?' Siggy came over to the sink. He picked up a dirty plate. Mr Ellis repeated his order. 'You clean. Understand?'

Sigurd gave a grin and nodded. 'I clean. I understand. I clean plips.'

'Not plips – plaps. No, I mean plates,' said Mr Ellis wearily, and he went off to clear the tabletops.

'I clean plaps,' muttered Siggy to himself, looking round the kitchen. He gathered up an armful of dirty crockery, opened the washing machine and put it all inside.

'Clean plaps very quick, easy peasy,' said Sigurd as he switched the machine on. He pulled up a chair and sat down to watch.

The machine filled with water. It began to rotate. The plates started to clatter against one another. Something broke. Something else cracked. The machine stopped. Siggy stared at it. He was about to open the door, when the things inside rotated the opposite way. There was a dreadful clatter and scrunch. An awful grinding noise came from the machine, along with the merry sound of tinkling glass and dozens of plates breaking into tiny pieces.

Sigurd sprang to his feet. This was certainly not meant to happen. He shouted at the washing machine. 'No, no! You clean, you clean plaps!' He punched the controls helplessly and started the spin programme. Faster and faster whirled the crockery, while Sigurd tugged at his beard in anguish.

Just as Mr Ellis came running to the kitchen to see what all the noise was, Siggy opened the machine door. Fragments of china came flying out at high speed, along with several gallons of soapy water. Mr Ellis screamed, raced to the power plug and switched off. The machine ground to a halt.

Siggy stood up in a deep puddle, from which poked a hundred bits of broken plate, sticking out like the hulls of sinking ships. He bent down and picked up a fragment. He looked at it dolefully and said with some sadness, 'Plaps gone small.'

'I'll give you plaps, you overgrown hairy meatball!' shouted Mr Ellis. 'Look what you've done! Look!' He seized a carving knife and began to advance on the Viking, who backed towards the door. 'Get to your room at once and stay there! Don't you dare come out until I say so. Do you hear? Now MOVE!'

Whether Siggy understood the words, or just reacted to the knife, it's hard to say, but he ran up the stairs four at a time and barricaded himself into Room Twelve.

The episode with the washing machine was followed by a big conference within the Ellis family. Mr Ellis kept saying that Sigurd would have to go: they simply couldn't afford to keep him in the hotel, which was losing enough money already.

Zoe and Tim were almost in tears, especially when their mother said she thought their father was right. 'Too many things go wrong when Sigurd's around,' she added.

'But where will he go, Mum?' Zoe sniffed. 'You can't put him out on the street.'

'No,' snapped Mr Ellis. 'But we can jolly well put him on a boat and send him back to Denmark.'

Everyone stopped and stared at Mr Ellis. 'Don't look at me like that,' he said. 'I'd like to know why not? That's where he came from. He rowed over here – he can bloomin' well row back. Come on!'

A strange procession made its way down to the beach. Tim and Zoe tugged at their father, trying to get him to change his mind. Mrs Ellis kept repeating that it had to be done. Besides, Siggy would be so much happier at home in his own country. As for Siggy himself, he didn't know what all the shouting was about, and was much more interested in all the boats in the harbour. He pointed at them and said a lot in his own language.

'See?' said Mr Ellis. 'He wants to go home.' He

fished a handful of money from his pocket and paid
for the hire of a large rowing boat.

'How long for, mate?' asked the owner.

'How long does it take to row to Denmark?'
muttered Mr Ellis darkly.

'What's that?'

'Just keep the change,' snapped Mr Ellis. He
pushed Sigurd into the boat and thrust the oars at
him. 'There. Denmark is that way,' he said, pointing out across the open sea. 'Start rowing!'

Siggy nodded happily and grabbed the oars.
This was wonderful. 'Siggy go home. Hedeby!
Goodbye, so long, how do you do!' The boat slowly
moved out through the first few waves. 'I go. No
more plaps. No more bathpoo.'

'Shampoo,' Zoe corrected tearfully. The rowing
boat was now some distance away, and steadily
getting smaller. Its path through the waves was a
bit crazy, but it was moving out of sight.

'Bye, Siggy,' whispered Tim. Zoe reached down and held her brother's hand tightly.

Mr Ellis watched grimly until the rowing boat was out of sight. Penny Ellis slipped an arm round his waist. 'Do you think he'll be all right?'

'Of course. He's a Viking – born to the sea. Those Vikings sailed to North America, right across the Atlantic Ocean. This time tomorrow, he'll be safe at home.'

Mrs Ellis sighed. 'You know, in a strange way, I shall miss him.'

'I won't,' grunted her husband, and they made their way back to the hotel.

On their return, Mrs Tibblethwaite came hurrying down the front steps to meet them.

'There you are! I am so glad you're back. Now, there's a family in the lounge. They want to know if you have any rooms vacant, as they wish to stay for two weeks. I must say, they seem very nice. And there are children, so Tim and Zoe will have people to play with. They're very excited and dying to meet Sigurd.'

'Sigurd?' repeated Mr Ellis. 'What do you mean, dying to meet Sigurd?'

'They saw him in Flotby, standing on a car roof and waving a sword. They seem to think it was some kind of advertising stunt. I told them he was a real Viking: they don't believe me, of course, but they will as soon as they meet him. Anyhow, the children are pestering their parents to let them stay at the hotel with the Viking, so here they are. But where's Siggy? They won't wait much longer, you know.'

Mr Ellis slumped into a chair and closed his eyes. He couldn't believe his bad luck. Surely this couldn't be happening to him? When he opened his eyes, the first thing he saw was Tim and Zoe watching him, their faces full of accusation.

He leaped to his feet and raced down to the beach. 'Siggy!' he yelled. 'Come back! You can come back, Siggy – please!' Mr Ellis stared out across the grey water to the endless horizon. There was nothing to be seen but waves and a few gulls circling slowly in the empty sky.

6

A Present from Thor

How do you explain to four excited children and their parents that you have just got rid of a real Viking? Mr Ellis winced and began. 'You see, we did have a real Viking. His name was Sigurd and he arrived from nowhere. We don't know how or why. Mrs Tibblethwaite found him in her bed. Then he hid in the cupboard, you see . . .' his voice trailed away. The story sounded so unreal, he could hardly believe it himself. Mrs Ellis carried on.

'He put the cups and saucers in the washing machine, drank gravy by the boatful and stuck the soap on his helmet, so we put him in a rowing boat and now he's rowing back to Denmark.'

'By himself?' asked Mrs Tibblethwaite in surprise. 'Really, Mr Ellis, I'm rather shocked.'

'It wasn't an advertisement then?' interrupted Mr Johnson.

'No.'

'He was a real Viking but we can't see him because he's rowing to Denmark?'

'Yes.'

'And you expect us to believe all that?' Mr Johnson sat and grinned at them all. 'Come on, you're joking, and it's a pretty good joke too.'

Mrs Tibblethwaite grunted and drew herself upright. 'It is no joke, Mr Johnson. I believe it because I know it is true, and I expect you to believe it too. I have been staying at this hotel for a week, and so has Sigurd. I know him very well.'

Mrs Johnson stifled a giggle. 'Oh I see – Mr Sigurd is your husband?'

'Of course he isn't!'

'But he was in your bed?' Mr Johnson added.

'Yes, I mean no – yes! Look, are you calling me a liar?' demanded Mrs Tibblethwaite angrily.

'No,' replied Mr Johnson. 'But you might be a nutcase. Surely you don't really think this character was a real Viking?'

Mrs Tibblethwaite sat down in despair. Mr Ellis started to say that obviously nobody was likely to believe them. Perhaps it was best if the Johnsons left. After all, Sigurd had gone.

He was half-way through this speech, when there was a heavy thudding and a clatter from the hallway. It sounded as if half an army had just broken down the front door and ridden into the hall. Zoe was about to go and investigate when the door burst open and Siggy squelched in. He was soaking wet and clutching a long piece of rope that trailed out of the room. Several bits of seaweed flapped about the horns of his helmet.

'Siggy!' cried Zoe, hugging him, even though he was wet.

'Siggy, Siggy!' Tim yelled, climbing up his dripping leg. 'Yuk!' he added and quickly let go.

'It's the Viking!' screamed all the children.

'How do you do, good evening, it's a lovely yesterday,' said Sigurd, beaming from ear to ear beneath his beard. 'I go row Hedeby. I row and row, round and round. Boat go this way, boat go that way. Where am I? Only water, no land, can't see. I stand up to see better. One oar go away.'

'What does he mean, "One oar go away"?' asked Mrs Johnson.

'He lost an oar,' Zoe said quickly. 'Go on, Siggy. Then what happened?'

'I row and row, one oar, I go round in circle, only smaller. I stand up again...'

Mr Ellis groaned. 'Don't tell me, you lost the other oar.'

Sigurd shook his head and drops of sea-water sprinkled from his beard. 'No, I keep oar, but fall into sea, splishy-splashy. Climb into boat but boat fall over, slopsy-wopsy. Boat sink. I sink. Gurgle-gurgle.'

'Good grief, who taught this idiot to speak?' moaned Mr Ellis.

'I swim. I reach land. I come here.' Sigurd stopped and grinned madly at everyone. 'I bring present. Present for Mr Ellis and Mrs Ellis.'

'A present?' repeated Mrs Ellis weakly.

'To say thank you and how are you,' explained

Siggy. He hauled on the rope in his hand. There was a strange clumping noise beyond the door. Sigurd pulled harder and at last brought into the room a large black and white cow. It stood there next to the settee like an alien from a distant planet, watching everyone with vast, moony eyes.

'This for you,' Sigurd said to Mr Ellis. 'Present from Thor, God of Thunder. We make offering.' Siggy pulled Nosepicker from his scabbard. 'Tonight we kill cow to say thank you for safe return and I not drown.'

One of the Johnson children was hiding behind her father. The youngest one was holding his nose and pulling at Mrs Johnson's sleeve.

'Mummy, mummy, I think that cow has just done a . . .'

'Yes dear,' interrupted Mrs Johnson quickly. 'I know.'

'Tonight we have feast,' Sigurd went on. 'Lots to eat. Yummy.'

Mr Ellis sighed heavily. A few minutes earlier, he had wished Sigurd was still with them. Now the Viking was back and already Mr Ellis was wishing he'd gone down with the boat, gurgle-gurgle.

'Zoe, please take Siggy and that cow outside,' he said. 'Explain why we can't sacrifice cows, and for goodness sake find out where this one came from. Take it back before some farmer slaps us all in jail. I shall try and sort out things here.'

Mr Johnson had started to laugh. He got up from his chair and seized Mr Ellis by the hand, pumping it warmly. 'I have an apology to make. I certainly do believe you. That Siggy must be a real Viking, couldn't be anything else. He's either a Viking or the biggest banana-brain I've ever met. Anyhow, I think it's fantastic. Question is, have you got a room for my family? We'd love to stay with a real Viking, wouldn't we?'

Mrs Johnson looked at the mess on the lounge floor. 'Only if the cow goes.'

Mr Ellis hastily began to push the bemused cow backwards out of the room. 'Of course, no problem. This cow hasn't paid its bill for weeks, anyway,' he joked.

Mrs Tibblethwaite let out a long sigh while Mr Ellis and Zoe rushed off to fetch keys and prepare beds. She could see how busy they were, so she quietly set about cooking supper for everyone.

By the time bedtime arrived, the Ellis family were exhausted. Mr Ellis kissed his children good night. 'I have an apology to make, too. I'm sorry I put Sigurd on that boat.'

Zoe hugged her father tightly. 'That's all right, Dad. He's come back to us, hasn't he?'

'He certainly has,' said Mr Ellis.

By the time morning arrived, Mr Ellis had done some serious thinking. He had spent half the night discussing plans with his wife. They had a big new family staying at the hotel, and that meant a lot of extra work. This time they would really have to train Siggy to do some of it.

'After all,' said Mr Ellis, 'it wasn't his fault that he put the washing-up in the washing machine.'

'Maybe not,' his wife smiled.

'We'll train him to be a waiter. We always need extra hands when it comes to dishing up food. Tim and Zoe will be back at school, so they won't be able to help much longer.'

The big plans were put into operation as soon as Sigurd appeared downstairs. Everybody was already at breakfast and Mr Ellis had warned them that Sigurd was going to help. 'Please be patient. He has a lot to learn.'

The smallest Johnson child poked his father's leg. 'This is going to be fun, Dad!'

Siggy appeared with two plates of scrambled egg and toast.

'That's for Mr and Mrs Johnson,' said Mr Ellis. 'Now, watch me, Siggy.' Mr Ellis carried a plate over to Mrs Tibblethwaite and put it in front of her. Sigurd grinned and took his plates across to the Johnsons. He tipped the contents on to the place mats. *Ssplopp!*

'Oh dear,' murmured Mrs Johnson.

'Siggy, you have to leave it on the plates,' explained Mr Ellis.

The Viking shook his big hairy head. 'No, make plaps dirty. No want dirty plaps.'

'It's okay, it doesn't matter if they get dirty. We always keep our food *on* the plates. Understand?'

'I understand,' said Siggy and he began to pick up the scrambled egg with his fingers and smear it back on the plates. The smallest Johnson tittered.

'He's funny,' he said.

'He's yukky,' the oldest one said, with some disgust.

'Sorry about this,' said Mr Ellis hastily. He

pulled Sigurd into the corner of the room and started hissing instructions at him. Mrs Tibblethwaite tapped Mr Ellis on the shoulder.

'Let me do this. You get back to the kitchen. I'll soon have him under control.'

Mr Ellis retired gratefully to the kitchen, while Mrs Tibblethwaite slung a tea-towel over one arm and grabbed the Viking with the other. 'Now, watch me,' she ordered, and Sigurd followed her like a lamb.

Mr and Mrs Ellis and Tim and Zoe watched spellbound from the kitchen. 'You know, I do believe the old girl is quite enjoying herself,' said Mr Ellis. 'They make quite a pair, don't they, Penny?'

'She's a bit like a Viking warrior herself,' his wife suggested. 'I'll be sad when she goes. She's been so helpful – more like one of the staff than a guest.'

Mr Ellis smiled. 'Maybe everything is going to be all right after all. Perhaps Siggy will bring us good luck.'

'He's brought us a cow already,' Tim pointed out.

Zoe started to laugh.

7

Vanishing Act

Mrs Tibblethwaite was having remarkable success with Sigurd. She bossed him about like nobody's business, but the Viking smiled and laughed and nodded. He was soon well on his way to becoming a star waiter. Meanwhile Mrs Tibblethwaite was often to be seen wearing Sigurd's helmet. She looked quite the part.

The two weeks of Mrs Tibblethwaite's stay passed all too quickly. Mr and Mrs Ellis did not want the stout lady to go, as she had proved so helpful around the hotel. Tim and Zoe were both very fond of her because although she often had a strict and bossy manner, her heart was as soft as a king-size duvet.

And when Sigurd discovered that Mrs Tibblethwaite was leaving, he went to pieces completely. He tore at his hair, stamped up and down the stairs, frightened all the guests with his shouts and raging. Nobody understood a word he said: it was all in his own tongue. He would not lift a finger to help in the hotel. In short, the Viking had gone on strike.

Mrs Tibblethwaite was upset as well. She did not like to see Sigurd so unhappy, so she sat

upstairs in her bedroom and tried to knit a jumper
to take her mind off everything. The idea did not
seem to work very well, as she ended up with the
only jumper in the world that had three arms, no
neck and a sock attached to one sleeve.

'Can't Mrs Tibblethwaite stay?' pleaded Zoe.

'It's really up to her,' explained Mrs Ellis.

'Can't she work here?' Zoe went on. Her mother
stopped and looked at her in surprise.

'I don't know, Zoe. It never occurred to me. I
don't suppose she would want to work here. She's
got her own home, hasn't she?'

Even so, Mrs Ellis became very thoughtful after
Zoe's suggestion, and decided she would talk to her
husband about it as soon as possible. But there
were other problems that needed seeing to first. All
the chickens had disappeared from the kitchen
table.

Mrs Ellis was certain she had taken three chickens from the fridge, ready to roast for lunch. When she couldn't see them, she decided her husband must already have put them in the oven to roast. When Mr Ellis couldn't find them in the fridge *he* had thought *she* must have put them in the oven.

It was now almost lunchtime, and they both went to the oven to get the chickens. But the chickens weren't there. They had quite disappeared. Mr and Mrs Ellis looked at each other and said the same thing at the same time. 'Sigurd!'

They raced upstairs to his room, where they found the Viking moping on his bed. Mr Ellis hauled him to his feet. 'Chickens! What have you done with all the chickens?'

'Chickens,' repeated Sigurd. It was not a word he knew.

'Yes – chickens!' roared Mr Ellis frantically. He began to strut up and down the room with his fists tucked under his armpits and his elbows waggling. 'Parrk parrk paarkk!'

Sigurd's eyes grew wider and wider. He took off his helmet and scratched his head. Mrs Ellis hurriedly joined her husband. 'Parrkk puk-puk-puk-puk-puk parrkk!'

'Chickens!' cried Sigurd suddenly with a big smile, and he nodded feverishly.

'Thank goodness he understands,' panted Mr

Ellis. But the Viking was now on his hands and knees, and had begun to crawl round the room.

'Woof wuff-wuff rrrroooff!' Sigurd looked up at Mrs Ellis with his tongue hanging from his mouth. 'Rrrroooffff!'

'I don't believe it. He thinks this is a game,' moaned Mr Ellis. He grabbed Sigurd and pulled him on to his feet. 'Sigurd, chickens, where are they? We want to eat. Eat chickens. Lunchtime. Understand?'

'Ah, chickens. Yum-yums. I give to gods for offering. I give chickens to gods in Valhalla. I say, Oh Gods be good and Mrs Dufflecoat no go away.'

'WHERE ARE THE CHICKENS!' screamed Mr Ellis.

Sigurd paused and regarded Mr Ellis coolly. 'I show you,' he said calmly, and marched downstairs. He took them outside and pointed up to the porch roof. This had a triangular front, with a wooden spike at each corner. There was a farm-fresh oven-ready chicken stuck on each spike.

Mr Ellis was about to break into a war dance when he saw the expression on Sigurd's face. The Viking was gazing upwards, his eyes half closed, his arms raised to the heavens.

'Hear me, Odin!' the Viking cried. 'Hear me, Thor! Hear me all the gods in Valhalla! Take my small offering and speak to the heart of Mrs Dufflecoat so she no go away. Speak to the hearts of Mr Ellis and Mrs Ellis and Tim and Zoe, who look after me, so they no send Mrs Dufflecoat.' Sigurd slowly lowered his arms.

Mrs Ellis gave a small nod and led Sigurd back indoors. 'I'm sorry,' she murmured. 'I didn't understand. Go back upstairs, Sigurd, and we'll cook beefburgers instead.'

Mr Ellis was suddenly taken by an idea. He went straight to Mrs Tibblethwaite, explained the problem and asked her how she would solve it. Mrs Tibblethwaite looked him in the eye and said that the answer was perfectly obvious: 'You offer me a job and I say yes, then I stay here and everyone is happy.' And that was how Mrs Tibblethwaite came to work at The Viking Hotel.

As for the chickens, they stayed up on the porch roof for a very long time. Zoe explained that it was quite normal for Vikings to make offerings like that: 'Usually it was a pig or cow, I think. We learned about it at school.'

Whether it was the chickens on the porch roof,

Sigurd or Mrs Tibblethwaite, nobody could be sure – but more and more people wanted to come and stay at The Viking Hotel. The hotel was soon doing great business, with all rooms full and booked for months to come.

The summer season ended with the great Flotby Viking Carnival. People all over the town had been preparing for weeks. It was a grand event, with parades along the streets, bands playing and a Viking Feast in the evening. There was dancing too.

Sigurd was like a small child. When he first saw the streets filled with Vikings, he thought Ulric Blacktooth had found him at last. He sat at the front window, watching with a pensive, faraway look in his eye. Zoe sat down beside him. She thought he would be excited and happy, today of all days. This was quite unexpected.

'You're thinking about home, aren't you, Siggy?'

'Hedeby,' grunted the Viking. Seeing all the people dressed like Vikings made his heart ache. Zoe left him to think alone.

Later in the evening they all went down to the harbour, where the grand feast and dance were to take place. Riding the waves in the harbour was a small boat, all done up like a Viking longship. It had shields along the sides and a striped sail. It even had a dragon's head prow (made from painted egg-boxes). Sigurd gazed at it with a curious smile and said, 'Baby boat,' which made everyone laugh. They went into the dance and left Siggy standing by the harbour, looking out to sea.

'He'll be all right,' said Tim.

'I'll go and have a word with him,' said Mrs Tibblethwaite. 'I'll see if I can get him to come and have a dance.' She set off along the harbour wall.

It was over an hour later that Mr Ellis suddenly realised he hadn't seen either Sigurd or Mrs Tibblethwaite come into the hall. Everyone had finished eating already, and there was no sign of them. His heart missed a beat as the truth came to him. 'Zoe, Tim, Penny! Quick, follow me!'

They pushed through the dancing crowds and out into the warm summer air. A brief glance at the harbour told them all they needed to know. The Viking longship had gone. They raced along the harbour wall and stared out across the dark sea.

'Nothing,' muttered Mr Ellis. 'I can't see a thing.'

'There! Over there, right on the horizon!' yelled Zoe. Far, far out to sea was a tiny sail. They watched it as long as possible, until it became a speck and then nothing.

The Ellises walked back to the hotel in a deep silence. On the porch steps they stopped and looked up at three very tatty old chickens.

'Give them a safe voyage, Odin,' said Mr Ellis quietly, and they went inside.

It was well past midnight when there was a loud knock on the front door. Mr Ellis went down in his dressing gown. Outside were two extremely wet figures. One was short and stout, the other was tall and hairy.

'We went round and round,' grinned Sigurd.

'He can't sail for toffee,' giggled Mrs Tibble-thwaite. 'He's totally hopeless. First of all...'

'He lost an oar,' butted in Mr Ellis. 'Don't tell me.'

'Big waves, very wet,' said Sigurd. 'Sail come down.'

'He was underneath, of course,' Mrs Tibble-thwaite put in. 'Then he struggled to get out and he couldn't see what he was doing and kicked me over-board...'

'Gurgle-gurgle,' grinned Sigurd. 'Sail go dropsy-flopsy. Mrs Dufflecoat make big splash. She make very, very, *very* big splash.'

'Yes, well that's quite enough of that, Sigurd. You made a big splash, too.' Mrs Tibblethwaite turned back to Mr Ellis. 'He fell in as well, of course.'

'Gurgle-gurgle,' added Mr Ellis. 'Come on inside, the pair of you.' He began to switch on the hotel lights. 'Penny! Zoe! Tim! Come downstairs. We have some important guests who have just arrived.'

Sigurd stood in the hallway, with a large puddle

of sea-water collecting round his feet. 'Tomorrow I make offering to thank gods in Valhalla for safe return,' he said.

'That will be fine, Sigurd,' said Mr Ellis. 'You can have a slice of bacon and no more. We haven't got any pigs, sheep or cows, so a slice of bacon will have to do.'

Sigurd stood and grinned at everyone like a huge, happy child. Suddenly he grabbed Mrs Tibblethwaite and gave her an enormous kiss. 'Sigurd like Mrs Dufflecoat. Like very much.'

'Oh – Siggy!' Mrs Tibblethwaite had turned bright red.

'Me love you!' declared Sigurd, with his idiotic smile. Then he grabbed her once more.

'All right, that's enough,' said Mr Ellis. 'Stop it at once. Time we ended all this.'

Viking in Trouble

This is for 'Berserkers' everywhere

1

Trouble Ahead

The Viking Hotel in Flotby was famous throughout
Britain – not for its fine cooking or excellent
sea-views – but because it had a real Viking living
and working there. People came from far and wide
to see Sigurd. He was, after all, quite a sight. He had
a fiercesome black beard and moustache and
somehow managed to draw attention to himself
wherever he went. This may have had something to
do with the way he waved his huge sword
'Nosepicker' about his head.

Nobody was quite sure how Sigurd came to be in
Flotby at the end of the twentieth century, but Siggy
had a strange story to tell.

'I from Hedeby in Denmark. I sail with
Ulric Blacktooth. Sit on boat long time and get dead
bottom. Big war fleet. We come to kill everyone and
steal everything. But mist come like cloud of

darkness, all spooky-wooky. Boats go in mist, can't see, like helmet slip down too far. We listen to sea. I sit at front of ship and ship go bang-bang against rocks. I fall off. Splash. Very wet, very cold. I get up. Where boat? Boat gone. I climb up cliff. I come to house. Agh! It's me! Outside is sign with me – Viking Hotel. I walk in. Here I am. I am Sigurd from Hedeby in Denmark. Good morning and welcome! Hot baths in every room. Very well thank you. The toilets are over there. Goodnight!'

At this point Sigurd would bow to his audience and there would be much applause. He had told this story many times. After all, he had been living at The Viking Hotel for almost a year now. Poor Mr and Mrs Ellis, the owners of the hotel, had been driven quite mad by him.

The problem was very simple. Siggy had come straight out of the tenth century and into the twentieth. A lot of things had changed since 900AD, and Siggy was still trying to get used to them. Meanwhile Mr and Mrs Ellis were still trying to get used to *him*.

The Ellis's children, Tim and Zoe, thought that Siggy was marvellous. They enjoyed showing him off to their friends and Zoe had even undertaken the hard task of trying to teach Sigurd some English.

Then there was Mrs Tibblethwaite, the widower who had first come to the hotel as a guest, but had stayed on – and on – and on. It wasn't much of a secret that Siggy was madly in love with her, or that Tibby, as she was affectionately known, had a very large soft spot for the daft Viking. It seemed quite obvious that they would get married.

The decision bit was simple, but after that it got very complicated and very noisy.

'We have Viking weeding!' announced Sigurd.

'Wedding, not weeding,' corrected Zoe.

'Ah! Viking wedding!' shouted Siggy, waving Nosepicker above his head and slicing through the lampshade. There was a loud bang as the hotel electrics fused and everything went dark.

'Who am I?' bellowed Sigurd, crashing into a near-by table.

'Not "Who am I?". You say "*Where* am I?".'

Mr Ellis heaved a deep sigh and made his way to the fuse box. A few minutes passed and the lights came back on. Siggy was on his feet in an instant, wildly waving his sword. 'Where did that? Sigurd kill him!'

'There's no need to kill anyone Sigurd. And you don't say "Where did that?" You must say "*Who* did that?".'

'Who did that?' Sigurd repeated slowly.

'Who did what?' asked Mr Ellis, coming back into the room.

Siggy looked at Mr Ellis, then at Zoe, and tried to puzzle out the new turn in the conversation. It was too much. His eyes narrowed to dark slits. 'I kill him!' he hissed.

'Kill who?' asked Mr Ellis, completely mystified.

Mrs Tibblethwaite could stand it no longer. She rose majestically to her feet and bellowed at everyone. 'That is quite enough of this gibberish. Perhaps we can get back to making the arrangements for the wedding. We shall have a church wedding, with a vicar and a white dress and a veil.'

Tim giggled and whispered to his sister. 'I didn't think vicars wore white dresses with veils.'

'Sssh! That's not what Tibby means.'

Zoe's reply was almost drowned out by the noise of Sigurd clambering on to a dining table. 'By Odin!' he thundered, 'I say we have a Viking weeding. We kill ten sheep, five cows, eight pigs and forty chickens. We make fire for Thor to bless our weeding. Then you Viking woman.'

Mrs Tibblethwaite hitched up her skirts and climbed up on the table beside her future husband. 'Just a moment, Sigurd. We are not going to sacrifice anything. I shall have a white weeding dress – oh bother you! I mean a white wedding dress, and we will be married in a church by a vicar or we won't be married at all.'

70

'Viking weeding!' bellowed Sigurd, waving Nosepicker alarmingly close to the light again.

'Church!' screeched Mrs Tibblethwaite, stamping her foot on the table. All of a sudden there was an almighty crash as the table collapsed beneath their weight. Sigurd and Tibby vanished from sight, emerging seconds later as a struggling heap on the ground.

They clung to each other as they struggled back to their feet.

'All right, you win Siggy,' laughed Mrs Tibblethwaite. But the Viking bowed low to her.

'We marry in church,' he said. 'I am yours forever.'

Tim turned away in disgust. 'Yuk!' he muttered. 'I think I'm going to be sick.'

Having finally agreed on the arrangements for the wedding, Sigurd and Mrs Tibblethwaite went to visit the vicar. Everything was going fine until the vicar asked Sigurd what his surname was.

'Surname?' repeated Sigurd, completely bewildered.

'Yes. My surname is Buttertubs. What is yours?'

'Buttertubs?'

'Ah – so your name is Sigurd Buttertubs. That's quite unusual for a Viking, I think.'

Mrs Tibblethwaite butted in. 'Of course his name isn't Buttertubs. He doesn't know what you are talking about. Do you think I'd marry anyone called Sigurd Buttertubs? If he has to have a surname call him 'Viking'. It's as good as anything else.'

And so the marriage of Sigurd and Mrs Tibblethwaite went ahead. Tibby got her wish and arrived in a flowing white wedding gown and veil. Sigurd got his wish too. Halfway through the ceremony he threw a pile of twigs on the church floor, set them on fire and raised both his arms.

'Hear me Thor,' he thundered. 'Bless this wedding. Make Mrs Tibblethwaite happy. Make . . .'

Sigurd's touching speech was brought to an abrupt end as the vicar frantically baled water out of the font and over the fire. There was a loud hiss, followed by clouds of smoke and the guests ran coughing from the church and headed straight for The Viking Hotel to begin the celebrations. Mr Ellis opened several bottles of champagne. Siggy seemed to think that the delicate little glasses were just *too* little to drink out of. He seized a water jug and threw the contents to one side.

There was a startled squeak. 'Eeek! I'm soaked! I'm flooded! My new dress!' cried the vicar's wife, as she stared open-mouthed at her soaking dress.

Sigurd was crestfallen. 'Very sorry, I make you better,' he said and began to brush down Mrs Buttertubs with his huge hairy hands. At once she started screaming again.

'Eeek! Get off me you brute! Don't touch me or I shall call the police! Help – police!'

Mrs Ellis came to her rescue. She guided Sigurd away and went back to help Mrs Buttertubs recover. Meanwhile Sigurd had opened two more bottles of champagne, poured them into the water jug and was sitting in an armchair. He gazed lovingly across the room at his new wife and raised his jug of champagne to her.

'Ears!' he shouted.

'Ears?' muttered Mr Ellis. 'Ears?'

Zoe giggled quietly. 'I think he means "cheers" Dad.' Mr Ellis began to laugh. Soon everyone was going round the room saying 'Ears!' to each other and raising their glasses.

Then some bright spark started saying 'Legs!' instead. The laughter got louder and louder.

The only silent person now was Sigurd, who was completely baffled. Zoe sat down next to him, tears rolling down her cheeks. She tried to explain, but every time she began she was overcome with laughter.

Nobody saw the small thin man in the dark suit enter the room and glance round suspiciously. He spoke seriously to each guest in turn until at last he came to Mr Ellis.

'Excuse me,' he said, in a voice that sounded as if it came from inside a very small tin can. 'But my name is Mr Thripp. I have been staying at your hotel for the last four days.'

'Jolly good,' laughed Mr Ellis. 'Hope you're enjoying yourself.'

Mr Thripp pressed closer. 'Actually, I can't say that I have. You see Mr Ellis, I work for the Health Department. I have been very concerned to see that the meals in this hotel are being served by one of the filthiest, dirtiest, most disgusting waiters I have ever seen in my life.'

By this time Mr Ellis was on red alert. 'Just what do you mean, Mr Thripp?' he demanded.

'I mean that so-called Viking of yours. He is a public health hazard. He is revolting. I am going to have to report this hotel to the Health Department, which means that unless you do something about him straight away, you will be closed down. Good day, Mr Ellis.'

The thin man slipped away through the guests like a slug through leaves. Mr Ellis stood quite still, the colour gone from his face and the enjoyment of the last few hours completely forgotten.

2

Taxi!

When Mr Ellis told everyone about the Health
Inspector's visit, they were all understandably upset
. . . especially Sigurd . . . 'I not dirty!' he cried,
banging both fists on his chest. Clouds of dust
erupted from his furry top and several moths decided
it was time to leave.

Mrs Tibblethwaite sat down, a fierce look in her
sharp eyes. 'It's no use panicking. We shall have to
work something out. What exactly is the problem?'

Mr Ellis sighed deeply. 'The problem is that if we
don't find Siggy another job the hotel will be closed
down and we shall go bankrupt.'

Tibby looked surprisingly cheerful. 'I really
don't see what all the fuss is about. The answer is
quite clear. We take my dear husband out of the
kitchen and give him something else to do.'

'Like what?' asked Zoe.

'Making the beds? Gardening? Cleaning rooms?' suggested Mrs Tibblethwaite.

Mr and Mrs Ellis looked at each other thoughtfully. It hadn't taken long to teach the Viking how to wait at table. Maybe he could be taught how to do something else. Mr Ellis stood up.

'Right then Siggy, how would you like to be a chambermaid?'

'Dad – he can't be a chambermaid! He'll have to be a chamberviking!' giggled Tim. Mr Ellis smiled. Sigurd looked puzzled.

'I want you to clean the bedrooms, Siggy. Understand?'

'I understand. I clean beetroots.'

'Not beetroots – bedrooms. Mr Johnson is leaving Room Nine. I want you to get all the bed linen from his bed and take it to the laundry room, okay?'

'Okey-dokey boss,' Sigurd replied as he disappeared up the stairs leaving a bewildered Mr Ellis staring after him.

'Where on earth did he learn to say "okey-dokey boss"?'

Tim turned bright red and hurried off to find something to do, leaving Mr Ellis to draw his own conclusions.

Upstairs, Siggy had reached Room Nine. He banged on the door and when there was no reply he marched straight in. Mr Johnson was still there, lying under the duvet, fast asleep. Sigurd bent over the unfortunate guest and shouted at him. 'Hey you! I clean beetroots. I clean today. You get up and go away!'

Mr Johnson stirred and groaned. 'What? What's going on? Look, I've got a stinking headache and I don't have to leave for another hour. Leave me alone. I'm going back to sleep.'

But the Viking wasn't having any of this. Mr Ellis had told him to collect the bed linen from Room Nine and that was exactly what he was going to do. Sigurd pulled out Nosepicker and pointed it at Mr Johnson. 'I clean beetroots!' he hissed.

'All right, go and clean beetroots if you have to, but leave me alone.' Mr Johnson sighed and turned over with a large groan.

Sigurd stared down at the poor guest. He pushed Nosepicker back into its scabbard and gritted his teeth. He reached down and grabbed all four corners of the bottom sheet. With one almighty heave he hoisted all the bedding, duvet and all, on to his shoulders, with Mr Johnson trapped inside and struggling to free himself.

'Hey! What's going on! Put me down you oaf!'

'I tidy!' shouted Siggy, stomping triumphantly downstairs.

'You're not tidy, you're filthy!' came a muffled voice from inside the duvet. 'Now let me out. Help!'

Mrs Ellis was the first to hear the cries coming from the back of the hotel and she hurried round to see what was going on. She was greeted by the sight of Sigurd striding into the laundry with a huge sack on his back. It was wriggling and shouting and had arms and legs popping out from all directions.

'Siggy? What is going on?'

The Viking grinned. 'I clean beetroot. This Room Nine.' So saying, he let the bundle fall to the floor.

'Ouch!' Mr Johnson struggled from the sheets, and after falling down three times because his feet were caught up, finally stood up in front of Siggy, red-faced and fuming. 'You idiot!' he yelled. 'You numbskull! Peabrain! Noodlebonce!'

Siggy stepped backwards as Mr Johnson marched towards him. 'I've never been in such an hotel!'

Mrs Ellis hastily tried to calm things down. 'I'm terribly sorry, Mr Johnson. Sigurd doesn't quite understand the rules of the hotel yet,' she said apologetically. 'Come with me and I shall make sure we give you a big discount on your bill.' As she took Mr Johnson gently by the arm and led him away she glared back at Sigurd. 'And you wait there and don't move!'

As soon as Mrs Ellis had finished with Mr Johnson she went off to find her husband. There was more serious talking to be done. 'I just can't cope with it all Keith. I am not going to spend the rest of my life giving our guests discounts because of that totally dopey Viking.'

Mr Ellis gave his wife a comforting hug. 'Don't worry. I think I've come up with a pretty good plan.' Penny Ellis glanced at her husband. 'You know how I've always complained about fetching and carrying guests to and from the station? Well, I thought I might teach Sigurd how to drive, and then he can do all that for us!'

'Are you sure Keith? I mean do you think Siggy could cope?'

'Of course, no problem! He'll love it. He'll take to it like a duck to water.'

'I just hope you're right,' murmured Mrs Ellis, already foreseeing disaster.

Siggy's first lesson was in the hotel carpark. Mr Ellis had taken the precaution of making sure there were no other cars parked there. Sigurd sat in the front seat looking terribly proud. He was quietly making 'brrrm brrrrm' noises into his beard and grinning madly at Mrs Tibblethwaite, who was standing by the back door watching.

'Think of it like a boat,' suggested Mr Ellis helpfully. 'This steering wheel controls the rudder.'

Sigurd appeared mystified. 'No oars. No sail. No boat. No float.' Mr Ellis wiped his forehead.

'No, well, perhaps not,' he said, beginning to wonder if teaching Sigurd to drive had been such a good idea after all. He took a deep breath. 'Listen, this wheel here makes the car go where you want it to. Understand?'

'Okey-dokey boss,' grinned Sigurd.

'Now, turn the key and start up the engine.' Mr Ellis pointed to the ignition switch. Sigurd gave the key a twist and the engine burst into life. So did Siggy. He shouted with delight and clapped his hands, bouncing up and down on the seat and going 'brrrm brrrrm' all over again. Mr Ellis tried to ignore him.

'This is the handbrake. Take it off like this. Put your foot on the clutch and push it down. That's right. Now we put the gear lever into first gear. See that other pedal? That's the accelerator pedal. Push it down gently and take your other foot off the clutch and weh-hey-whoa-ooohaaaargh. . . !'

Suddenly they were off.
In a giant series of leaps and
bounds the car began to spring
across the carpark. Stones spurted
from the wheels and shot out behind,
showering Mrs Tibblethwaite. Mr Ellis
hastily grabbed the steering wheel and tried
to give the car some sense of direction. At last
the car stalled and came to an abrupt halt.
Sigurd threw open his door and leapt out
on to the carpark, where he began a madcap
dance of triumph. Even Mrs Tibblethwaite
joined in, while Mr Ellis sat in his car breathing
heavily and saying a few prayers of thanksgiving
for a safe delivery. All at once Siggy was back
in the driving seat.

'Again,' said the Viking. 'I go faster.'
'Steady on,' said Mr Ellis. 'Don't get too
excited. Right, start up again and
this time we'll go for second gear.'

'Second fear!' shouted Sigurd incorrectly.

'You said it,' muttered Mr Ellis as the engine came to life and the little car began bucking round and round the carpark. 'Put the clutch in,' yelled Mr Ellis above the roar of the overworked engine. 'Now put the gear lever into second gear.'

'Second fear!' cried Siggy again as the speed of the car increased by about twenty miles an hour.

'Slow down, Siggy! Take your foot off the gas! Slow down! Watch the corners! Change gear! Slow down! Turn left! No right! Left! Change gear! Steer! Watch that. . . !' Mr Ellis's voice trailed away to a helpless whimper as the car went charging round and round in circles that were getting wider and wider and faster and faster.

'Brrrm brrrm brrrm,' yelled Sigurd, grinning madly. Mr Ellis put his hands over his eyes. Never had 'second fear' seemed so real.

It was at this point that Siggy grew tired of going round and round in circles and yanked the steering wheel in the opposite direction. The turn was so sharp that the car almost turned right over. Mr Ellis was hurled against the side door and when he next looked straight ahead he was alarmed to see that they were now heading for the hotel garden. There was a sickening crunch as the car bounced up the kerb and then they were on the grass. Mr Ellis made a last attempt to grab the steering wheel and save them both, but it was too late.

'Brrrm brrrm brrrrm!' cried Sigurd once more as, with a final burst of speed, the car shot across the lawn and did a nose dive into the hotel pond.

'Water!' announced Sigurd. 'Splish splash! I get out now.' He climbed from his seat out into the pond and struggled to the shore. The car sank a bit deeper. Mr Ellis pulled himself from the passenger seat and followed the Viking back to the hotel.

Sigurd looked back at the sinking car with great disappointment. 'That car no good,' he said, shaking his head. 'It no float. Bad car. I go clean beetroots for Mrs Ellis.'

Mr Ellis watched him squelch into the hotel with a look of despair. He knew that Mr Thripp would soon be back, but for now he didn't have the energy to do anything about it.

3

Deathsnore!

It took the breakdown truck over an hour to pull the car out of the hotel pond. Thankfully, apart from the car being rather wet not too much damage had been done. The car wouldn't start of course, and had to be towed to the garage to be dried out. Meanwhile, the Ellises were still left with the problem of how to employ Sigurd.

Tim suggested that maybe Sigurd could carry guests' bags up to their rooms, but Mrs Ellis was not so sure.

'I think that half the problem is that Siggy doesn't know how to talk to people normally. After all, he does come from the tenth century. It must be so difficult for him.'

Her husband gave a half-hearted smile and kissed his wife on the cheek. 'You're so forgiving. Sigurd does all these awful things and you forgive him.'

'That's because he's locked in a time-warp. You're not, Keith, and if you don't get that hedge trimmed soon YOU certainly won't be forgiven.'

'Ah – well I've had a really good idea about that hedge,' began Mr Ellis. 'I am going to hand over the gardening to Sigurd. It's ideal for him. A bit of grass cutting, some hedge trimming and so on – just the job.'

Mrs Ellis was doubtful. 'You may be right Keith, but knowing Sigurd you probably aren't. Give it a try anyway. He can't be any worse at it than he was at cleaning the bedrooms. Goodness me – look at Mrs Tibblethwaite, she doesn't look very happy. I wonder what's up.'

Mrs Tibblethwaite was indeed very unhappy and quite unlike her usual self. She hurried over to Mrs Ellis. 'I don't know what to do. I just don't know,' was all she could say.

'Please Mrs Tibblethwaite, do try and keep calm,' said Mr Ellis. 'Whatever's the matter?'

'I've just had this awful telephone call. I don't know what to do. My sister, you remember, she came to the wedding – she lives in Scotland. Well, her next door neighbour has just telephoned to say she's had a nasty fall. She's been taken to hospital with goodness knows what broken.' She turned her pale face towards Mr Ellis. 'What am I to do?'

Mr Ellis took her hands and squeezed them gently. 'You go and look after your sister, Mrs Tibblethwaite. She needs you. Go to the hospital and make sure she's all right. Take as long as you wish.'

Mrs Tibblethwaite nodded gratefully. 'But what about the. . . ?'

'The hotel will be fine,' added Mrs Ellis.

'I mean Sigurd,' whispered Mrs Tibblethwaite.

'What about my husband? He's such a child!'

'Leave him with us. He'll only be in the way if you take him to Scotland. He'll be fine with us,' said Mrs Ellis, secretly crossing her fingers behind her back as she spoke.

'Yes, we'll look after him,' said Tim. 'He can teach me sword fighting with Nosepicker.'

'Hmmm, very useful that will be!' muttered Mr Ellis.

'Oh thank you, thank you. I was hoping you'd offer to look after him,' said Mrs Tibblethwaite. 'I'll go and pack straight away and catch the first train from Flotby,' and with that she hurried upstairs.

Mrs Ellis watched her go.

'Siggy will be fine with us,' she repeated. 'Oh dear, why *did* I say that?'

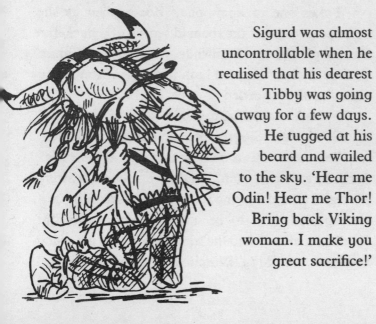

Sigurd was almost uncontrollable when he realised that his dearest Tibby was going away for a few days. He tugged at his beard and wailed to the sky. 'Hear me Odin! Hear me Thor! Bring back Viking woman. I make you great sacrifice!'

'She's only going for a few days, Siggy,' Zoe pointed out. 'You're such a fusspot. You can help look after the hotel instead.'

Sigurd stopped. He straightened up and whipped out Nosepicker and thrust it into the air. Unfortunately it stuck in the ceiling but it was still a grand gesture. 'I am Sigurd the Viking,' he bellowed. 'I swear by all the gods that I will defend the hotel until the great day when Viking woman returns!'

It was a stirring speech, but quite meaningless, and when Sigurd yanked out Nosepicker from the ceiling and brought down half a ton of plaster, everyone wondered whether they really wanted him to defend the hotel anyway. Tim looked across at Zoe and rolled his eyes.

'He's a complete nutter,' he whispered to her.

'Takes one to know one,' Zoe replied as she disappeared out of the room in search of a bucket to put the plaster in. Meanwhile, Mr Ellis took Sigurd outside to show him the high hedge that ran round the edge of the garden.

'It needs a good trim, Siggy.'

'Good trim?' Siggy repeated, a little bewildered.

'Yes. Look, this is a hedge trimmer. It's electric.' Mr Ellis switched it on. Sigurd leapt back drawing Nosepicker and waving it violently at Mr Ellis as if he expected there to be a major battle. Mr Ellis laughed and switched the trimmer off. 'It's not going to attack you Siggy. Watch. This is how you use it.'

Mr Ellis switched the trimmer back on and began to slice neatly through the hedge. Twigs and leaves fell on every side. Sigurd watched closely. He thought this was marvellous. Mr Ellis put the machine into his hands and helped Sigurd guide the trimmer over the hedge.

'You see? It's easy with a hedge trimmer. Now, I want you to do the whole hedge, right the way round. Okay?'

'Okey-dokey boss.'

'I do wish you wouldn't say that,' said Mr Ellis as he turned to walk back to the hotel. But just as he was about to step inside, he heard the roar of the hedge trimmer and felt a sudden uneasiness. 'Do try and make a good job won't you, Siggy?' he said desperately.

'I make good job,' muttered Sigurd, as the hedge trimmer vibrated in his hands. Mr Ellis went into the hotel. He couldn't spend all day worrying about Sigurd – he had some plastering work to do.

For several moments Sigurd just stood there, marvelling at the wonderful machine that Mr Ellis had so carelessly placed in his raving Viking hands. A murderous glint came into Siggy's eyes and he looked wildly about the garden. The engine roared and Sigurd began to advance on the enemy.

Back in the hotel, the first person Mr Ellis saw was Mr Thripp. The thin little Health Inspector was back, complete with his tin-can voice. 'Good day, Mr Ellis,' he whined. 'I hope it's a good day for you?'

Mr Ellis managed a weak smile. 'Fine thank you, Mr Thripp. To what do we owe the pleasure of your company?'

'I have come about your "Viking". Not that he is a *real* Viking of course. I think it would be going too far to claim that.' Mr Thripp looked up sharply, his weasel eyes fixed on Mr Ellis.

'That's really no concern of yours,' replied Mr Ellis, trying to remain calm. 'Anyway, what can I do for you?'

'I have just come to make sure that this – "Viking" – is no longer a health hazard to your visitors, or I shall have to issue orders to close the hotel. I do hope he is no longer serving food?'

'Of course not. He's working in the garden,' replied Mr Ellis.

Mr Thripp gave a sneaky smile. 'You won't mind

if I check on that will you? It's not that I don't believe you. It's just that . . .'

'. . . you don't believe me,' finished Mr Ellis. 'Follow me, Mr Thripp, and you will see that Sigurd is quite harmless.'

The two men walked out into the garden. They stopped. They stood still. There was no garden. From the far corner could still be heard the murderous whine of the hedge trimmer as Sigurd sliced through the last few flowers, bushes, shrubs, hedges – in fact anything that was more than a few centimetres tall.

Mr Ellis could barely speak. 'What have you done?' he croaked. Sigurd gave a broad smile and switched off the hedge trimmer.

'I cut hedge like you show me! Zzzipp! Zzzapp! This better than Nosepicker. When Sigurd next go to war he take Deathsnore.'

'Deathsnore?' repeated Mr Ellis in a trance.

'I call new weapon Deathsnore. It make noise

like man snoring and bring death to everything –
Deathsnore.'

Mr Ellis began to mutter to himself. 'I've got a
mad Viking in my garden who has just destroyed
every bush and flower with a hedge trimmer called
Deathsnore. What am I going to do?' He was so
overcome by the full-scale destruction of his garden
that he didn't notice Sigurd's bulging eyes and
purple face. The Viking had just seen Mr Thripp.

'You kill my weeding!' roared Sigurd. 'Now I kill
you!' The hedge trimmer gnashed its teeth and
Sigurd plunged after the Health Inspector. Mr
Thripp gave a high scream and raced into the hotel,
locking the door behind him.

'I kill you!' bellowed Sigurd. 'You very little man.
I make you littler. I cut you into pieces like salami!'

It took Mr Ellis ten minutes to calm Sigurd and get Deathsnore away from him, and a further hour to calm Mr Thripp. The thin Health Inspector was shaking from head to foot.

'We shall see about this, Mr Ellis. I have never been threatened before and you needn't think that you will get away with it. He was going to chop me up with a hedge trimmer. I'm going straight to the police. That maniac should be in jail, and so should you. This hotel is a disgrace. It's not an hotel at all, it's a madhouse. You should all be locked up. I'm going to the police now. This isn't the last you've heard from Ernest Thripp. I shall be back, mark my words, and then there'll be trouble . . .'

The delirious inspector ran off down the hotel steps, shaking his fist and screaming at the top of his voice.

Mr Ellis slumped into an armchair and buried his face in his hands. 'If only this were just a bad dream,' he said to himself.

4

Sigurd Goes Berserk

Mr Thripp ran all the way to Flotby Police Station. 'Help, help! There's a Viking on the loose and he wants to chop me up like salami!' he screamed at the officer on the front desk.

Constable Pritty fixed Mr Thripp with a calm stare, 'I see, Sir. Would you like to take a deep breath and just tell me as calmly as you can what's happened?'

Mr Thripp glanced fearfully over one shoulder at the open door. 'I have just been to The Viking Hotel. There's a Viking there – at least there's a madman who says he's a real Viking and he tried to chop me up with Deathsnore.'

'Deathsnore? Excuse me sir, but what is Deathsnore?'

'A hedge trimmer.'

'A hedge trimmer?'

'Yes Officer, a hedge trimmer. For heaven's sake, open your ears and listen. You've got to do something about it.'

'This sounds very serious indeed, Sir. Attempted murder with a hedge trimmer. Can you describe the criminal?'

'Yes. He's revolting.' Mr Thripp said bluntly.

'Revolting,' repeated Constable Pritty. 'Do you think you could give me a few more details, Sir?'

'Yes. He's revolting, disgusting and filthy!' said Mr Thripp completely missing the point.

'No, no, Mr Thripp – can you describe what he looks like?' Quickly Mr Thripp described Sigurd more clearly. Constable Pritty was rapidly drawing on to a big sheet of paper as Mr Thripp spoke, and as soon as the Health Inspector had finished, Constable Pritty triumphantly held up his sketch.

'There! What about that? I don't think we shall have much trouble finding this lad. Of course it is quite impossible that he's a real Viking, so he's breaking the Trade Descriptions Act as well.'

Mr Thripp gave a sneaky smile. 'And he's a foreigner!'

'Foreign eh? We'd better check his passport then. He may be an illegal immigrant. Let's see, what have we got so far – attempted murder, contravening the Trades Description Act and being an illegal immigrant.' The constable licked the end of his pencil. 'Not to mention carrying an offensive weapon, namely one hedge trimmer,' he said, looking up triumphantly.

'I think your Viking chappie could be spending a long time in jail. Come on, let's go and arrest him.'

It was hardly a surprise to Mrs Ellis when she answered the knock on the hotel door to find Mr Thripp and a policeman standing there. The policeman pushed himself forward and adjusted his helmet. 'I'm Pritty, Madam,' he explained.

Mrs Ellis examined the policeman's young face carefully. 'Yes, I suppose you are pretty in a way – for a policeman that is.' The constable turned extremely red.

'That is not quite what I meant, Madam.'

'No, I don't suppose it was. Would you like to start again?'

'I am Police Constable Pritty and I am afraid
that I have come about a very serious matter. I have
come to arrest a Viking by the name of Sigurd.'

Mrs Ellis had never thought it would get quite as
bad as this. She could tell from the sickening smile on
Mr Thripp's face that there was big trouble in store
for Sigurd, and she had no idea how to rescue him
from this new situation.

'I'll fetch him for you,' she said quietly, and
hurried off to find her husband.

Mr Ellis gritted his teeth at the news. 'Sigurd's in
the garden planting some new bushes. I'll bring him
to the hall.'

A few moments later Mr Ellis arrived with Siggy.
His hands were covered in mud from the garden,
where he had been digging. Mrs Ellis introduced
everyone, hoping that Sigurd would make a good
impression on the policeman. Siggy knew all about
English good manners. He strode forward with a big
grin on his innocent face and shook Constable Pritty
warmly by the hand.

Unfortunately he left most of the hotel garden smeared across the constable's hand. The policeman gamely tried to wipe it off, only to put several large muddy streaks across the front of his uniform. 'Damaging a police officer's uniform – that's a very serious charge indeed,' muttered Constable Pritty, fumbling for his notebook.

Mr Ellis asked if there was a problem. Why did they need to arrest Sigurd? Constable Pritty immediately launched into a long description of all the charges, with Mr Thripp grinning and hopping excitedly from one foot to another and adding bits here and there. Finally Constable Pritty asked to see Sigurd's passport.

'Pass-the-pot?' repeated Siggy. Glancing round the hotel entrance he saw a rose bush standing in a big tub. Of course! That must be it! Sigurd seized the flowertub with both hands, picked it up and thrust it into Constable Pritty's chest. 'Pass-the-pot!' Siggy repeated excitedly, thinking this must be some new party game.

'What are you doing? Are you trying to be funny?' cried Constable Pritty. Sigurd nodded and grinned even more.

'I funny. You funny. Funny man in funny blue hat!'

Constable Pritty thrust out his chin and snapped at his helmet strap. 'I am not funny at all, and neither is my hat,' he growled.

Mr Ellis hastily came to Sigurd's aid. 'Sigurd doesn't have a passport, Officer. You see, it's not that he comes from another country, but that he comes from another century – the tenth century, and they didn't have passports then.'

'Oh yes? And my name is Darth Vader!'

'I thought he was taller,' murmured Mrs Ellis.

'This is not a laughing matter, Madam. This Viking will have to come down to the police station with me for questioning.'

Mr Ellis turned to Sigurd and tried to explain the situation to him, but Siggy would have none of it. 'I no go with Mr Blue-hat.'

'Insulting a police officer,' muttered Constable Pritty reaching for his notebook again. 'I'm afraid that you have no choice, Sir. Just come with me please and don't make things worse for yourself.'

It was at this point that Constable Pritty made a bad mistake. He tried to pull Sigurd along by the arm. In an instant Sigurd had leaped backwards, pulling Nosepicker from his scabbard as he did so.

'Hah!' yelled Sigurd. 'Death to my enemies and to the enemies of my enemies and the enemies of the enemies of enemies – I think. By Thor, I make you all into barbecue meat!'

It was no use trying to calm the Viking down now. His blood was up. He stood there waving Nosepicker over his head so violently that he cut down three hanging baskets. Constable Pritty and Mr Thripp stared in horror at the mad Viking warrior and slowly began to back down the path.

Constable Pritty was secretly delighted at all this. Flotby was such a boring town normally and now he had a full scale incident on his hands.

'I think reinforcements are called for,' he hissed to Mr Thripp. 'Come on, back to the station – fast!' The two turned tail and ran, leaving Sigurd standing on the hotel steps waving Nosepicker. Mr and Mrs Ellis looked desperately at each other.

By this time Tim and Zoe had come outside to see what all the fuss was about. When they heard that Sigurd was about to be arrested and taken away they were horrified.

'Do something, Daddy!' cried Tim.

'I can't. I don't know what to do,' wailed Mr Ellis.

'But he hasn't done anything wrong!' cried Zoe.

'No? What about chasing Mr Thripp with a hedge trimmer, not to mention trying to skewer a policeman with Nosepicker.'

'But that was self-defence,' argued Zoe.

'Smell the fence!' shouted Sigurd with a big grin.

'Not smell the fence – self-defence,' corrected Zoe. Sigurd nodded violently.

'Smell the fence!'

Mr Ellis buried his face in his hands. He could hear the wail of fast-approaching police cars. Tim stared out from the hotel steps. 'Quick!' he shouted. 'You've got to do a runner, Sigurd. They're after you.'

But Sigurd stood his ground. 'I no go. I no coward. If Blue-hat wants Sigurd he come and take him.' Sigurd slowly drew Nosepicker and strode to the front of the steps as six police cars burst on to the forecourt. Doors sprung open and twenty police officers leaped from the cars. Constable Pritty stood near the back with a megaphone.

'Give yourself up!' he shouted. 'There is no escape. You are outnumbered. It's twenty against one. Give yourself up!'

Sigurd's answer to this was quite extraordinary and took everyone by surprise. He started taking off all his clothes. He pulled off his boots. He pulled off his jacket. Then he removed his shirt and started on his leggings.

'What's he doing?' whispered Mrs Ellis.

'Taking all his clothes off,' said Mr Ellis, not quite believing what he was seeing. Zoe clutched at her father's arm.

'Daddy I know what he's doing! He's going berserk!'

'Berserk?' repeated Mr Ellis. 'He's stark raving bonkers if you ask me!'

'No, no! That's where the word berserk comes from. A "berserk" was a Viking warrior. When faced with terrible odds in a battle they took off all their clothes and then charged into the fight!'

'What an extraordinary thing to do, and what peculiar things you learn at school,' said Mr Ellis.

By this time Sigurd was sitting on the stone floor, pulling at his leggings and muttering to himself. 'I berserk warrior. I cover garden with blood of Mr Blue-hats!'

Seizing his chance, Constable Pritty shouted 'Charge!' and a line of twenty police officers pounded towards the steps of the hotel, while Sigurd desperately tried to make up his mind. Was he going to pull his leggings off, or pull them back on again?

5

Sigurd Makes His Escape

Yelling furiously because it made them all feel a lot braver, the policemen stormed the hotel steps. Sigurd struggled to his feet and pulled up his trousers. He waved Nosepicker violently. The police paused for a moment and watched the bare-chested Viking warily. Sigurd glared at each and every one with a murderous glint. Then suddenly he shouted 'Boo!', turned tail and vanished into the hotel.

'Charge!' squeaked Constable Pritty once more, and the police plunged after Sigurd, only to get completely jammed in the doorway. There was an awful lot of huffing and puffing and grunting and grumbling as they sorted out the pile-up. Then they were up and stumbling after the laughing Viking.

Sigurd was having a wonderful time. He raced up one staircase and reappeared at the top of a quite different set of stairs. He slid down the banisters, rushed through the kitchen, back into the hotel, up the stairs again, and in and out of the bedrooms causing astonished shouts from the guests. Then he went downstairs again, through the lounge, into the garden, up the fire escape . . . and all the time the number of people chasing him grew and grew, as guests came out of their rooms and joined in.

At last Sigurd decided he had done enough running. He cast a quick look over his shoulder to watch the long blue snake bobbing up and down on his trail, then he dipped along a short corridor and vanished, leaving nothing but a flapping door to show where he had passed.

Twenty policemen and fifteen guests ran panting into a small room only to find it completely empty. There was no sign of Sigurd apart from an open window. Constable Pritty rushed over and stared out into the garden. Siggy was standing down

there, waving to them all.

Constable Pritty gritted his teeth. There was no way he was going to leap down into the garden from this height. He rushed out to the stairs and raced down to the garden. Sigurd had vanished again. 'Search the place!' screeched the constable. 'He must be around here somewhere!' The policemen ran round and round the garden like escaped guinea-pigs, shaking their heads.

Mr and Mrs Ellis and Tim and Zoe knew exactly where Sigurd was and they couldn't bear to watch. Perhaps it was the terrible crashing of gears that finally gave the police the clue they so desperately needed.

A car engine whined furiously and, with a lot of wheel spin, one of the police cars suddenly rocketed from the hotel driveway. The siren blared and, with another ear-shattering scrunch of the gears, Sigurd whizzed out through the hotel entrance and on to the main road. Mrs Ellis covered her eyes. Tim and Zoe jumped up and down with excitement.

'Go on, Sigurd! Show them what you can do! Yeehah!'

The police watched in disbelief, until a frustrated cry from Constable Pritty sent them scurrying to the remaining cars. The air was filled with howling sirens, stones were catapulted from spinning wheels and five police cars set off in hot pursuit.

Slowly the sirens faded away and the dust settled on the hotel forecourt. Penny Ellis slipped one arm round her husband's waist. 'What happens now, Keith?' she asked. 'I don't think I can cope with much more.'

Mr Ellis stood staring out along the main road. At last he turned back to the hotel. 'I'm going inside. I'm going to make a pot of tea and I'm going to take three aspirins for my headache – that's what is going to happen next. Then we shall sit down and wait. I am quite certain that it will not be long before we hear from the police again.' Mr Ellis went wearily into the hotel. Zoe and Tim watched in silence as Mrs Ellis followed her husband. Tim looked up at his big sister.

'Trouble?' he asked.

'Big trouble,' said Zoe, and they sat down on the front steps and waited.

The car chase did not last long. Sigurd's driving had certainly not improved since he had taken Mr Ellis's car for a swimming lesson in the hotel duck pond. Before he had worked out how to steer he had driven straight down on to the beach. Startled holiday makers took to their heels, screaming in alarm, as the roaring, wailing police car bounced round and round and finally took off in a series of sand-churning zig-zags before plunging nose-first into the waves. Perhaps Sigurd thought this car might float and he could just carry on driving until he reached Denmark. Of course it didn't work. The car came to a full stop with an engine full of sea water. Sigurd opened the door, stepped straight into a large wave, fell over, choked, came up gasping and collapsed right into the arms of Constable Pritty, ably assisted by nineteen other officers.

Constable Pritty grinned. 'You're booked, my son!' There was a click of handcuffs and Sigurd was hauled away, bundled into a police car and whisked off to Flotby Police Station. The telephone call that The Viking Hotel was dreading came sooner than expected. Mr Ellis stood there with the telephone at one ear, grim-faced and looking very tired. It was Mr Thripp speaking from the other end, and he was obviously enjoying every moment of his triumph. At last Mr Ellis put the 'phone down. 'He's been locked in the cells. That's it. He doesn't stand a chance. The police don't take kindly to being threatened with swords and having their police cars stolen. What a mess! I don't know what to do now.' He slumped down in an armchair.

Mrs Ellis straightened up. 'I know what to do,' she said, going to the telephone. She dialled a long number which seemed to ring for ages before it was answered. 'Hallo?' said Mrs Ellis. 'Is that you, Mrs Tibblethwaite? It's Penny here. How is your sister?' There was a long speech from the other end, but at last Mrs Ellis said 'Oh good. I'm so glad she's making a good recovery. How is everything here? Well, we do have a little bit of a problem. Yes. Just a wee one. Sigurd is in prison . . .'

There was a yell of horror down the telephone that even Mr Ellis and the children could hear. On and on went the rantings and ravings. At length Mrs Ellis put the 'phone down and smiled across at her husband and children. 'Mrs Tibblethwaite is catching the next train to Flotby,' she announced.

'I don't see what good that will do,' said Mr Ellis gloomily.

'Well, put it this way, Keith. If you were Constable Pritty and you had just put Sigurd in a police cell, would *you* like to face Mrs Tibblethwaite and explain it to her?'

A slow smile spread across Mr Ellis's tired face. He kissed his wife on the cheek. 'You, Penny, are a clever and dangerous woman.'

'That's as maybe, but I'm not half as dangerous as Mrs Tibblethwaite when she's on the rampage!'

'Is there going to be a fight, Dad?' Tim asked. 'Can I join in? Is Mrs Tibblethwaite going to bash them all up?'

'Tim! That's not a nice way to talk at all!' interrupted Mrs Ellis. Tim sighed.

'I was only asking,' he grumbled.

'Well why don't you go and do something useful – like tidy your room – before we have to go and meet Tibby's train. Go on.'

Tim heaved another sigh and went upstairs. He tried tidying his room but he was far too excited. The next few hours of waiting were a nightmare.

But if Tim was bored with waiting at the hotel, it was nothing compared to the rage and frustration felt by Mrs Tibblethwaite as her train slowly made its way towards Flotby. She couldn't believe a train could move so slowly. When the ticket collector made his way down the carriage she even asked if he would like her to get out and push. He didn't think it was at all funny.

Mrs Tibblethwaite had spent the last few days nursing her sister, and already she felt that she had been stuck indoors for far too long, running backwards and forwards with cups of tea and hot-water bottles. She now had a great deal of unused energy, and as the train crawled into Flotby station the door was already open. Mrs Tibblethwaite leapt down on to the platform, suitcase in hand and galloped to the barrier where the Ellises were eagerly awaiting her arrival.

'Where is he? Where is my Siggy?' she cried.

Mr Ellis took her by the arm and steered her towards the car, which had only recently come back from the garage, not only working, but dry. As they all got in Mr Ellis told her the whole story.

Tibby sat in the back seat with tears struggling down her cheeks. She clenched and unclenched her fists, over and over again. Then she began to beat her knees with her fists and finally the back of the driver's seat. She nearly sent Mr Ellis through the front windscreen and the car over a red light.

'For goodness sake!' cried Mr Ellis. 'Be careful!'

'I'll kill that Mr Thripp! I knew it was all his fault. He's a mingy, mangy, mean little pipsqueak. I'll kill him!'

'That won't help much,' Mr Ellis pointed out. 'Listen. We'll go back to the hotel and have a nice cup of tea and sit down calmly and think it all through. What we need is a plan.'

6

The Bomb Falls

A cup of tea did little to calm Mrs Tibblethwaite. She sat at one of the dining tables drumming her fingers angrily on the polished surface. She hadn't even bothered to take off her coat. The Ellis's watched her, wondering what she was thinking, and what she was going to do.

Tim was the first to break the silence. 'Suppose we rush into the police station and shout "Fire! Fire!" Then everyone will come running out and we can nip in and rescue Siggy.'

'How do we unlock his cell?' Zoe demanded.

'We could saw through the bars.'

'Timmy! That's a crackpot idea.'

'Well you think of something better then – Brainybottom.'

Mrs Ellis threw a cold glance across the table at the children. 'Okay, that's enough, you two. We have enough problems without the two of you arguing.' Mrs Ellis turned to Tibby and patted her gently on the hand. 'Would you like another cup of tea?'

Mrs Tibblethwaite shook her head. It was plain to all that she was quietly seething inside, and they waited for her to explode. But she didn't. At last she pushed back her chair and picked up her handbag.

'I'm going down to the police station,' she announced. 'Mr Ellis, would you kindly give me a lift please?'

'What are you going to do?'

'I'm going to talk to them. I cannot believe that this policeman – Prettyboy, or whatever his name is – can be stupid enough not to realise what a terrible mistake has been made. I am quite sure it is all a simple misunderstanding. Come on. The sooner we go, the sooner this whole mess will be cleared up.'

There was no stopping Mrs Tibblethwaite now, so everybody piled into the car and Mr Ellis drove to the police station. Just as they expected Constable Pritty and Mr Thripp were both there. They were sitting behind the front desk eating some large cream cakes and looking very self-satisfied. Beyond the desk could be seen a row of cells. One of them had a very sad looking heap of smelly rags piled in the corner.

Mrs Tibblethwaite marched up to the desk and rapped on it with her knuckles. 'I believe you have my husband, Officer, and I would like him back if you don't mind.'

Constable Pritty was nonplussed. 'I'm very sorry, Madam. You must be mistaken. The only person we have here is . . . hmmm!' Constable Pritty glanced at Mr Thripp and they both began to snigger. 'I can only describe him to you as being a raving madman, dressed in the smelliest, filthiest, most ridiculous clothes you've ever seen. He thinks he's a Viking! What a laugh! We do see some nutters in here, Madam.'

Mrs Tibblethwaite smiled back at the grinning policeman. 'That nutter *is* my husband, Officer, and for your information he is not mad. He *is* a Viking. Kindly release him.'

Constable Pritty and Mr Thripp stared at each other. Mr Thripp had a chocolate eclair stuck halfway to his mouth. Both men looked across at the Ellis's.

'She's telling the truth,' said Mr Ellis helpfully.

'God's honour!' added Zoe.

'Cross our hearts and hope to die!' Tim put in for good measure.

Constable Pritty leaned forward across the desk, unwittingly putting his elbow right on a cream doughnut. Jam and cream splurted out on all sides. 'Well, Madam, I am afraid your husband is facing some very serious charges.' And he went through the whole list, finishing with, 'stealing a police car and trying to drown it'.

'But he didn't know he was doing anything wrong. He's a tenth century Viking!'

'Oh of course Madam! And I'm Donald Duck!'

Mrs Tibblethwaite was rapidly running out of patience. 'It was all done in self-defence,' she said wearily.

At that moment the ragged heap in the far cell burst into life and threw itself at the bars. 'Smell the fence!' bellowed Sigurd, shaking his bars as hard as he could manage.

'My poor Siggy!' cried Mrs Tibblethwaite, stretching her arms towards her imprisoned husband. 'What have they done to you?' She turned back to Constable Pritty and fixed him with a steely glare.

'Please let him out, Constable – I'm sure we can settle the whole thing in court. He is perfectly harmless. There's no need to keep my husband like some caged-animal.'

'Harmless!' squeaked Mr Thripp, having finally managed to swallow the chocolate eclair. 'He threatened me with a hedge trimmer!'

'Let him out!' snapped Mrs Tibblethwaite.

'No.'

Mrs Tibblethwaite plonked her heavy handbag on the desk. 'Do you know what this is, Officer?'

'It's a handbag, Madam,' replied Constable Pritty very coldly.

'Wrong. It's a blunt instrument . . .' hissed Mrs Tibblethwaite as she whirled it round her head like a Viking axe. 'And I use it for hitting stupid policemen over the head until they see some sense.'

She began to batter Constable Pritty so hard that he had to duck down behind his desk, where he hurriedly pushed the alarm button. A siren screeched through the building.

Sigurd rattled his bars in fury. 'Let me out! Don't you touch Viking woman! By Thor, I'll ring your telephone!'

Zoe shook her head. 'I think you mean that you'll wring his neck, Siggy.'

'Yes, yes! I ring neck and telephone! Leave Viking woman alone!'

Why Sigurd was making such a fuss was a mystery to the Ellis's because Constable Pritty and Mr Thripp were getting by far the worst of the battle as Mrs Tibblethwaite continued to batter them with her handbag.

But reinforcements were now arriving fast from other parts of the police station, and soon a major battle was under way.

Tim jumped up and down and shouted 'Fire! Fire!' just in case it helped, which it didn't. The rest of the family retreated to the safety of the far corner and waited for the inevitable to happen.

It was amazing how strong Mrs Tibblethwaite was, and Mr Ellis wondered where on earth she had learned all her wrestling tricks. Policemen went flying in every direction. She had the head of one gripped under one arm and was busy giving an armlock to another. But the odds were finally overwhelming.

It was sheer weight of policemen that won the day. They piled on top of Mrs Tibblethwaite until there was a huge seething blue mountain. Out came the handcuffs and a few moments later Tibby was pushed into the same cell as Sigurd. They clung to each other in a touching embrace.

Constable Pritty picked himself up from the floor, straightened his hat, and tried to appear calm and unmoved. Tim and Zoe managed to stop themselves from telling him that there was a rather squashed chocolate eclair sitting on his right shoulder like some weird giant caterpillar. 'Any more of you like to be put behind bars?' he asked.

Mr Ellis slowly shook his head. He went to the cell and peered through at Sigurd and Tibby. 'Don't worry. We'll have to leave you here for the time being until the matter comes up in court. We'll see you at the trial. I'm sure everything will be fine!' he said, trying to sound reassuring.

Mrs Tibblethwaite was surprisingly cheerful. 'That's all right Mr Ellis. You go and look after the hotel. I've got Siggy and he's got me, and that's all that matters!'

For the next few days The Viking Hotel was filled with a deep and gloomy silence. Even the guests wandered about with clouded faces. The main reason the hotel had so many customers was because of Sigurd. They liked to see the huge, hairy Viking wandering about the place getting into trouble and speaking his very strange version of English. Now that he was no longer there they realised how much they missed him. Even Mr Ellis felt it although he was the one who always had to deal with the problems Sigurd caused.

They missed Mrs Tibblethwaite, too. She was central to the smooth running of the hotel. In fact Mrs Ellis thought that if Tibby had not had to go and look after her sister all these problems would never have occurred.

Mr and Mrs Ellis found themselves rushing about working three times as hard as they used to. Tim and Zoe helped out as best they could but it was no fun for anyone. There was immense relief when at last the day of the trial came. Everyone from the hotel, even the guests, made sure that they had front row seats at the Flotby Courthouse for the trial of Sigurd and Mrs Tibblethwaite.

Mr and Mrs Ellis had to give evidence. They tried to tell the judge that Sigurd was a Viking from tenth century Hedeby. They tried to tell her the story of how Sigurd had come to The Viking Hotel in the first place.

The poor judge was obviously very confused, but it was Zoe who finally managed to convince her that the story was true. She spoke with simple honesty, about their life with Siggy over the last year and she told Judge Farley how she had taught Sigurd to speak and had learned about his home.

Judge Farley was very impressed and things seemed to be going well for Sigurd and Tibby. Then Constable Pritty and Mr Thripp took the stand and things went from bad to worse. Crime after crime was mentioned, the last one being 'causing a chocolate eclair to stick to a police officer's uniform'.

The Ellis's watched Judge Farley's face closely. It was getting sterner by the second. From time to time she glanced across at Sigurd and Mrs Tibblethwaite with a deep frown. She shook her head slowly and scribbled notes on her note-pad.

Mrs Ellis slipped her hand into her husband's and whispered to him. 'I don't like it, Keith. Look at the judge's face. I'm afraid Tibby and Sigurd are really for it this time.'

7

Here Come The Vikings!

'Sigurd of Hedeby,' began Judge Farley, 'you have been charged with several very serious offences. I have listened most carefully to all the evidence against you and it is quite clear that these crimes have taken place.'

Mrs Ellis gripped her husband's arm tightly. 'I told you – he's in for it now,' she whispered.

'Ssssh,' muttered Mr Ellis as Judge Farley continued.

'It is also clear to me that if I were a Viking warrior, hundreds of miles from home, in a strange country and, even worse, in a strange *century*, I might well have behaved in the same way, especially if I had come across Constable Pritty and Ernest Thripp.'

By this time the entire Ellis family were sitting on the edges of their seats, nervously grasping the hand rails in front. Judge Farley coughed and went on, while Constable Pritty and Mr Thripp slowly turned paler and paler.

'In the normal course of events the behaviour of these two men would have been quite correct. They both have jobs to do, and they were both doing them. But these events were *not* normal. They were faced with something that they simply could not understand. It was their own reactions that drove Sigurd, and Mrs Tibblethwaite to behave as they did. I therefore find both of the defendants NOT GUILTY.'

A huge cheer almost tore the courtroom apart. The hotel guests leapt up and down, laughing and kissing each other. Zoe, Tim and Mrs Ellis were all in tears and Mr Ellis sat silently shaking his head, unable to believe the verdict. The judge banged her hammer loudly to bring back some order.

'There still remains one problem which must be dealt with as soon as possible. Mr Thripp was quite correct to report Sigurd for handling food. The guests at The Viking Hotel may enjoy the novelty of being served by a Viking, but I am quite sure that they wouldn't enjoy a dose of food poisoning. It is most important to find Sigurd something harmless to do and I order that this must be done by the end of the week.'

So saying, Judge Farley rose and swept out of the courtroom, leaving Sigurd's supporters to carry on cheering and to dance their way out on to the streets of Flotby. A conga of excited guests swept up the High Street and back towards The Viking Hotel, while Sigurd and Mrs Tibblethwaite sat on the roof of the car and waved to the laughing crowds as they made their way home. Sigurd had actually asked if he could drive – Mr Ellis had flatly refused.

'Talk about nerve,' he muttered to himself.

Back at the hotel the party continued for a long time. Siggy was even allowed to drink champagne from a water jug. Zoe brought down some of her music tapes and soon the guests were dancing around the tables in the dining room. Siggy joined in, clomping around, and became so excited that he got Nosepicker out and seconds later it was firmly stuck in the ceiling – again. Siggy thought it was so funny he left it there.

'It's like King Arthur and the sword in the stone,' suggested Tim. Tibby threw her arms wide open and shouted across the room.

'Hear ye! Whoever pulls this mighty Nosepicker from the ceiling will be the future King of England!'

Everyone collapsed laughing, ate far too much food and dragged themselves off to bed exhausted.

The following morning there seemed to be an awful lot of headaches around. Mr and Mrs Ellis eyed each other gloomily across the breakfast table. 'I still don't know what we can find Sigurd to do,' complained Mrs Ellis. 'The judge said it had to be something harmless. That's impossible with Sigurd.'

Tim came marching into the room holding Nosepicker aloft. 'I am the future King of England!' he announced loudly.

'Ssssh,' murmured Mr Ellis. 'Can't you see we're suffering? Anyway, we are trying to think of something for Siggy to do.'

'Maybe Mrs Tibblethwaite can think of something,' said Zoe.

'After the way she battered those policemen the other day I'm beginning to wonder if she's as safe as she looks,' said Mr Ellis. 'The pair of them strike fear into the heart!'

Tim put down Nosepicker with a loud clunk. 'I've just had a thought,' he said.

'Stand-by everyone!' giggled Zoe. 'Tim's had an idea!'

'But it's a good one,' said Tim. 'I think Siggy and Mrs Tibblethwaite ought to become wrestlers.'

'Wrestlers?'

'Yes – wrestlers.'

'WRESTLERS?!'

'Like you see on television sometimes, a tag team. They can dress up like Viking warriors. They'd be brilliant.'

There was complete silence round the table. Zoe was about to burst out laughing when Mrs Tibblethwaite walked in. She was moving carefully and slowly, as if the soft pile of the carpet was unbearably painful to her feet. 'I feel as if there's a road drill inside my head,' she said. She sat down slowly. 'Why is everyone looking at me?' she asked.

'Tim thinks that you and Siggy ought to be tag team wrestlers,' said Zoe with a little laugh. Tim stuck his tongue out at her. Zoe smiled and stuck hers out too. Mrs Tibblethwaite held her throbbing head in her hands and looked across at Tim.

'Just at this moment I don't think I could wrestle a pillow and win. But when I am feeling better, Tim, you and I are going to sit down and have a long chat. I think you are a genius. It's the most exciting idea I have heard for ages. Now, if you don't mind, I shall go back to bed until the roadworks inside my head have finished.' Tibby got up and slowly left the room.

Mr and Mrs Ellis and Zoe stared across the table at Tim, who had a quite ridiculous grin across his entire face. 'I'm a genius,' he reminded them all, picking up Nosepicker once more. '*And* the future King of England!' Zoe snorted and stamped out of the room.

Days passed in a whirlwind of activity. Posters went up all over the town. They were in shop windows, on lampposts, on cars, everywhere. The lettering was bright yellow and black and there was a colour photograph of Sigurd and Mrs Tibblethwaite in full Viking wrestling gear.

In a large empty room at the hotel, Sigurd and Tibby practised hard. Their first match was coming up fast, and they were up against one of the country's top tag teams, Grabbit and Grind. The two Vikings worked very hard and by the time the day of the wrestling match arrived they felt they were ready for anything.

Flotby Hall was packed out. It seemed as if everyone in the town had come to see the local celebrity and his wife in their first wrestling bout. The Ellis family had front row seats, and were barely able to control their excitement. They were astonished to see that Constable Pritty, Mr Thripp and Judge Farley were all in the audience.

A great cheer swept through the crowd as the main lights went out and the spotlights came on. There was a fanfare of trumpets and Grabbit and Grind appeared. Then another huge cheer went up as Sigurd and Tibby marched down to the ring. 'Yeeehah!' squealed Tim, and the bell pinged for the first round, Sigurd up against Grabbit.

First of all they circled each other, then there was a thunderous bang as they crashed into each other. Their arms locked and their muscles bulged. They grunted and heaved and hurled each other round the ring.

Zoe covered her eyes with her hands and then hastily uncovered them because she couldn't see anything. The wrestlers changed over. Grind threw herself at Mrs Tibblethwaite and they both fell to the floor. 'Go on Tibby,' screamed Zoe, beating her fists on her legs. Mr Ellis leaned back a calm smile on his face. He slipped an arm round his wife's shoulders.

'Who'd have thought it would end like this?' he whispered to her. 'Look at those two in the ring. They are having the time of their lives. Tim was right and it was a brilliant idea. We've solved the hotel problem too. We shall have even more customers now thanks to Sigurd and Mrs Tibblethwaite. Even Constable Pritty and Mr Thripp seem to be enjoying themselves. It's wonderful.'

The bangs and thuds went on as Sigurd and Mrs Tibblethwaite battled away with their opponents. Sigurd was standing on the ropes, both arms raised to the ceiling. 'By the God Thor!' he yelled. 'I telephone your neck!' he bellowed at Grind.

'Telephone your neck?' repeated Mrs Ellis to Zoe.

'I think he means he wants to wring her neck,' Zoe explained.

Sigurd launched himself from the ropes and landed on top of Grabbit. 'Now I make sacrifice to Thor!' he cried.

'Oh dear,' groaned Mr Ellis. 'It looks as if Siggy can even turn a wrestling match into a disaster area. I can't bear to watch!' And Mr Ellis screwed up his eyes tightly and shoved his fingers in his ears, whilst all around him people cheered wildly as The Viking Warriors grappled their way to victory.

Siggy and Mrs Tibblethwaite stood proudly in the ring, arms above their heads in triumph. Everyone cheered and clapped until their hands were sore.

'Dad, Dad,' cried Zoe tugging at her father's arm. 'It's all right, you can open your eyes now. Siggy and Mrs Tibblethwaite have won – they're a success!'

'A success,' muttered Mr Ellis, staring at Siggy with a look of amazement.

'I suck eggs,' Siggy shouted to him, hugging Mrs Tibblethwaite and grinning madly.

Mr Ellis looked at his wife in despair. 'Do you think he'll ever be normal?' he asked.

'I shouldn't think so,' she said. 'Anyway, what does it matter, Siggy's a success just the way he is.'

Mr Ellis looked doubtful, but left Siggy to get on with things in his own peculiar way. For now, at least, it seemed the best way of coping with the daft Viking.

Viking at School

1

The Biggest Wrestling Match
in the World

Mrs Tibblethwaite flew through the air, looking rather like an overstuffed rag-doll, and landed with an immense thud on the floor. She picked herself up and sighed groggily. It was strange being part of a top wrestling team. She stood and watched as a very large and scruffy Viking warrior zoomed over her head and crashed into the front row of the audience. Mrs Tibblethwaite sighed again. It was even stranger being married to a real Viking.

She climbed out of the ring and tried to pull Sigurd from the laps of three startled, elderly ladies, but they clung on to him and threatened Mrs Tibblethwaite with their bulging handbags.

'We're going to keep him!' screeched the lady with huge, horn-rimmed glasses.

'You can't keep him,' explained Mrs Tibblethwaite. 'We are in the middle of a wrestling match, and besides, he's my husband.'

'Well you can't have him,' insisted the lady with thick brown stockings, locking both her arms round Sigurd's hairy head. 'He belongs to us. We're his fan club.'

This was too much for Sigurd. The prospect of being carried off by three old age pensioners was a real blow to his pride. A Viking being kidnapped by women! It was unheard of! He was supposed to capture them! Sigurd leapt to his feet and scowled at the three old ladies. He'd show them!

'I kidnap you!' he cried. 'I take you home. Now I have three sleeves.'

The ladies looked at Sigurd, glanced at each other and shook their heads with bewilderment. 'You've only got two arms,' observed the horn-rimmed glasses, 'so how come you've got three sleeves?' But before they could say anything more Sigurd began to pluck them from their seats.

'You my sleeves!' he cried, tossing brown-stockings over his shoulder. 'You do anything I say!'

Mrs Tibblethwaite shook her head. 'I think you mean "slave" Sigurd, not "sleeve". Anyway, they can't be your slaves. That sort of thing isn't allowed any more.'

'We don't mind!' cried the three old ladies, hanging halfway down Sigurd's back. 'We love Siggy - he's our hero!'

Mrs Tibblethwaite shut her eyes and sat down on the edge of the wrestling ring. This was always happening. Whenever they appeared as one of the country's top tag-wrestling teams half the old women in the audience fainted and swooned. They threw their hankies at Sigurd, and their pension books. And they always tried to sneak off with him.

Suddenly, Mrs Tibblethwaite was brought
back to life by a loud and angry voice from above
her head. 'Oi! Are you two fighting us
or not?' shouted Bone-Cruncher
Boggis, leaning over the ropes.

He had a shiny, bald head
and he was wearing a black,
spangly leotard with 'MAD
AND BAD' written across
the front in silver letters.
He reached down with
a long, hairy arm and
grabbed Mrs
Tibblethwaite
by one ear.

'Ow!'

Sigurd dropped the three ladies at once and rushed across to help his wife. 'You leave my Tibby!' he cried. 'You nasty big belly!'

'Who are you calling a big belly?' demanded Monster Mash, Bone-Cruncher's partner.

'He means bully,' squawked Mrs Tibblethwaite. 'He's calling you a big bully. Ow!'

Sigurd was not going to put up with any more of this. He leapt into the ring and seized Bone-Cruncher by one leg, dragging him across the floor. Monster Mash threw himself on top of Sigurd and all four of them rolled round and round the ring, making various squashed and squidged noises such as 'Oof!' and 'Urrrff!'. Then Monster Mash jumped on top of Sigurd, and struck a triumphant pose. The breath came out of Sigurd's flattened chest like the air rushing from a whoopee cushion...

'Ssspplllllrrrrrrrrrrr!'

134

The three pensioners watched in dismay. Their hero was about to be beaten! In desperation, they clambered into the ring and started attacking Monster Mash and Bone-Cruncher with their handbags. 'Take that!'

'Leave Siggy alone!'

'Bullies!'

The poor referee tried to intervene, but he was quickly caught in the crossfire of several whirling handbags and sank to the floor unconscious. Other members of the audience hurried from their seats to join in the battle. Some of them were fans of Monster Mash and Bone-Cruncher and it was not long before the entire wrestling ring was filled with noisy, struggling bodies. After a few minutes, the fight spilled out beyond the ropes, on to the floor, up the aisles and amongst the audience.

Then the police arrived - all four of them. It wasn't enough of course and they sent for reinforcements. Thirty more policeman hurried to the scene. But that wasn't enough either. By now, the entire audience were at each other's throats. Even more reinforcements were sent for and eventually the Fire Brigade arrived and hosed everyone down. That stopped the fighting, but it didn't stop the quarrelling.

'Who started it?' demanded Inspector Hole, tipping a litre of water out of his hat.

'He did!'

'No - she did!'

'It was the Viking!'

Fingers pointed in every direction, but mostly they pointed at Sigurd. He crawled out from beneath a squelchy pile of bodies, looking rather bedraggled. Inspector Hole sized him up cautiously. Oh yes! Here was the culprit if ever there was one.

'Dressing up as a Viking eh?' he sniggered. 'That's a bit childish, isn't it?'

Mrs Tibblethwaite bristled. 'He's a real Viking,' she snapped.

'Oh yes? And how's that then?' the inspector smirked.

'Sigurd sailed to England in a Viking longship with a raiding party a thousand years ago. He got separated from the others, went through some kind of Time-mist and ended up in our time; now he's my husband.'

Inspector Hole wrinkled his nose. 'Sounds like you've been watching too many fantasy films,' he muttered. 'Right then, let's see - causing a disturbance - that's about five years in prison. Fighting in public, assault, starting a riot, damaging property - and didn't you say he was some kind of raider? That's definitely not allowed nowadays. Must be another forty years or so...'

'You can't send him to prison!' cried Mrs Tibblethwaite.

'Yes you can!' shouted the referee. 'He's a menace to society - they both are. If it hadn't been for them this would never have happened. Look at my Wrestling Hall! It will cost thousands of pounds to repair all this.'

Inspector Hole fished around in his pockets for a pair of handcuffs. Sigurd looked most upset. 'I good boy,' he muttered.

'Yes he is,' agreed one of the pensioners. 'It wasn't his fault, officer. If you try and send him to prison we shall complain to the Police Authorities.' Sigurd grinned cheerfully at Inspector Hole.

'They my sleeves,' he explained somewhat confusingly.

Inspector Hole heaved a deep, deep sigh. It was obvious the crowd would make trouble if he tried to arrest the Viking and his wife. 'Okay everyone,' he grumbled. 'The fun's over. You'd better all go home before I decide to make a mass arrest.'

The referee was beside himself. 'Aren't you going to do anything?' he demanded. 'My hall is ruined.'

'Nothing I can do I'm afraid,' said the inspector, but the referee wasn't going to put up with this.

'Okay. If you won't do anything, I will.' He fixed Mrs Tibblethwaite and Sigurd with a stern eye. 'You two are banned,' he declared, 'and not just in my wrestling hall, but anywhere in the world. You'll never wrestle again. You're banned for life!' The ref turned and stalked back inside his sodden hall.

Inspector Hole grinned maliciously. 'Well, it looks like you two are out of a job,' he sniggered. 'Serves you right,' he added as he got into his car and drove off. The Fire Brigade packed away their hoses and drove off. Slowly, the crowd began to squelch back to their homes. Even the three old ladies shuffled away, quietly crying into their cardigans.

It took a little while for Sigurd to understand what had happened. 'No more bish-bash?' he asked. Mrs T. shook her head. 'No more squish-squash?'

'No,' said Mrs Tibblethwaite.

'No more leg-wrinkles and head-crinkles?'

'NO!' shouted Mrs Tibblethwaite impatiently.

'You cross,' he observed.

'Yes! I'm cross!'

'You very cross.'

'Yes! I'm very cross!' cried Mrs Tibblethwaite.

'You very, very, VERY cross!' said Sigurd.

'Oh for goodness' sake shut up!' yelled poor Mrs Tibblethwaite, and she belted Sigurd so hard with her handbag that it stuck on one of his helmet horns.

As he struggled to pull it off, the clasp on the bag opened and half her belongings tinkled out through the hole.

Mrs Tibblethwaite wearily got down on her hands and knees and began to pick everything up. 'I wish you understood how serious this is, Siggy,' she told him. 'We shall never be able to wrestle again. We have no work, and that means we have no money. How are we going to live?'

Sigurd looked at his wife with a cheerful grin. 'Easy-peasy, Japanesey,' he said. 'We go see Mr and Mrs Ellis, and Tim and Zoe. We go back to Viking Hotel and God's your ankle!'

'Bob's your uncle,' corrected Mrs Tibblethwaite, before falling into silent thought. Go back to The Viking Hotel? Perhaps that would be the best thing to do - at least for the time being. Mind you, Sigurd was such a handful. He always seemed to bring trouble wherever he went. Mrs Tibblethwaite wondered what Mr and Mrs Ellis would think about the return of the Viking.

2

A Severe Case of Vikingitis

Zoe and Tim were delighted. They could not think of anything better than having Sigurd back at The Viking Hotel. They hurtled down the front steps of the hotel and launched themselves at the new guests.

'Tibby!' cried Zoe.

'Siggy!' yelled Tim.

'May the good Lord save us all,' murmured Mr Ellis to his pale wife.

He put on a brave smile and marched down the steps towards his uninvited guests. 'Sigurd - how nice to see you again after all this time. How are you?'

'How are you to you two too!' beamed Sigurd.

Tim burst out laughing. 'He sounds like an owl, doesn't he Zoe? Doesn't he sound like an owl? Too-wit, too-hoo, wooty-too, tooty-wooty-hooty...'

'All right, Tim,' said Mrs Ellis. 'I think we get the picture.' She turned to Mrs Tibblethwaite, took her suitcase from her and immediately ground to a halt because she couldn't manage the weight. Mrs Tibblethwaite picked it up with one hand. 'What's all this about?' asked Penny Ellis. 'This is a surprise.'

Mrs T. gave her a sharp look and nodded. 'I thought you might not be too pleased,' she sighed.

'Oh, it's not that...' Penny trailed off in confusion as her cheeks turned a delicate and embarrassed red. Mrs Tibblethwaite patted Penny's arm.

'It's quite all right. I thought you might be a just a touch apprehensive about Siggy coming back here, but I'm afraid my dear that we had little choice.'

'We thought you were on another wrestling tour,' said Mrs Ellis.

'We were on a wrestling tour. Unfortunately things got a little out of hand at our last match...'

'How surprising,' murmured Penny, with a knowing glance at her friend. 'I don't suppose it had anything to do with Sigurd?'

'Of course it did, but it wasn't really his fault.'

'It hardly ever is,' Mrs Ellis pointed out. 'It's just that he's always there when things go wrong.'

'Quite,' sighed Mrs Tibblethwaite. 'Anyway, to cut a long story short, we have been banned from wrestling in public ever again, so we are both out of a job. We didn't know what to do...'

'So you came here,' finished Penny and Mrs Tibblethwaite nodded glumly. 'Don't worry,' Penny went on brightly. 'You are very welcome - although I am not so sure about Siggy! Just look at him out in the garden with Tim and Keith.'

The two women peered out through the window. Sigurd seemed to be giving Tim lessons in swordsmanship. Tim was staggering round trying to lift Nosepicker above his head and going cross-eyed with the effort.

'You have to be like wild animal!' shouted Sigurd. 'You roar and stamp and scare your enemies! You rush at them and go Rraaaargh!'

'Sigurd,' interrupted Mr Ellis. 'Do you think you could look where you're going? You're treading on our new flowers. I only planted them last week.'

But Sigurd was far too busy showing Tim how fierce a real Viking warrior could be. 'I show you. You watch me. I scare panties on all enemies.'

'Siggy! You have to scare
the pants off your enemies,
not on them!' Tim giggled.
Sigurd seized Nosepicker from him.
'Raaargh!' he yelled, whirling the
fierce blade round his head like a
helicopter about to take off. 'Raaaargh!'
'Mind out!' cried Mr Ellis. 'You've just
chopped my new forsythia bush in half!'
'Death to forsythia!' yelled Sigurd,
taking another great swipe.
'It's only a bush, Siggy. It's not your
deadly...argh! Help!' Mr Ellis
suddenly set off round the garden
as Sigurd leapt after him, growling
and scowling and waving
Nosepicker like a giant
carving knife.

Round the garden they went, five times, until at last Sigurd stopped, put his hands on his hips and burst out laughing.

'You see me, Tim? I scare his panties all over the place.'

Mr Ellis collapsed exhausted on to the garden bench. His wife came out with a tray of tea and biscuits. 'Are you having fun, dear?' she asked gently. 'Playing Vikings with Siggy and Tim?' She winked at Mrs Tibblethwaite and Zoe. Poor Mr Ellis couldn't answer at first. He was too busy panting.

'That man's a maniac! He could have killed me! Will he be staying long? Oh I do hope not. I don't think I could cope. We've enough problems with the hotel as it is.'

'Oh please, Dad!' pleaded Zoe. 'Let him stay a bit. It's fun when Siggy's around.'

'Fun?! Look at this place! That Viking has only been here ten minutes and already the garden looks like the surface of the moon!'

'I'm afraid Siggy might be here for some time,' said Mrs Ellis. She handed him a cup of tea and explained about the wrestling ban. Her husband's face crumpled at the news. Mrs Tibblethwaite hastily reached inside her bag, pulled out a little silver flask and unscrewed the cap before offering it to Mr Ellis.

'Drink this. It's brandy - strictly for medicinal purposes. I usually have a drop or two when I find myself suffering from Vikingitis.

Mr Ellis took a few gulps, coughed, spluttered and sat up straight. Colour flooded back to his face. The children watched him carefully.

'Please!' mouthed Zoe.

'You've got to let Sigurd stay or I shan't speak to you ever again!' scowled Tim.

'Is that a threat or a promise?' asked Mr Ellis. 'Okay, Siggy can stay for a while, but there are certain rules. Number one: no swords, indoors or outdoors. Number two: you both have to help in the hotel.'

'We'll do anything to help,' said Mrs Tibblethwaite.

'I help,' beamed Sigurd. 'You no want sword? Okey-dokey. I throw sword away!'

'Sigurd! No!'

But Sigurd had already hurled Nosepicker over one shoulder and the mighty sword was flying through the air. Five seconds later, there was an almighty crash of splintering glass as it smashed through the hotel greenhouse. Mr Ellis seized Mrs Tibblethwaite's silver hip-flask, took another deep swig and buried his head in both hands.

After that things quietened down a little. This was partly because Mr Ellis took to his bed with a headache and various other symptoms of Vikingitis, while Mrs Tibblethwaite and Siggy got settled into one of the hotel bedrooms.

The only other guests at the hotel were an elderly couple, the Ramsbottoms, and Mr Travis, who was in Flotby on business. The truth of the matter was that since Sigurd had left business had gone down. While there had been a real tenth-century Viking staying at the hotel it had attracted customers. But when Siggy and Tibby became a tag-wrestling team and began their country-wide tour many of the hotel guests left, and had not returned.

The Viking Hotel was beginning to look a bit tatty. What it really needed was a good coat of paint. The Ellises had already decided they ought to do the painting while there were so few guests staying and Mr Ellis reckoned that Sigurd could make himself useful with a paintbrush. Early the next day he set the Viking to the task. 'Do the front of the house first of all,' said Mr Ellis, leaning a ladder against the front porch. 'I want all the doors done, and the windows and the railings. Understand?'

'Okey-dokey boss,' nodded Sigurd, levering the lid off the paint tin. There was a loud SCROYYOINNGG! and the lid whizzed across the road like a flying saucer and landed upside down on Mr Crump's front doorstep. Mr Ellis sighed and went back inside.

Sigurd quickly warmed to his task. The paint was a lovely bright green. Up and down the ladder he went, singing away to himself one of the songs Tim had taught him, but with new words.

'Siggy Viking had a brush;
slip-slap, slip-slap-slop!
And on this brush
he had some paint;
slip-slap, slip-slap-slop!
With a plip-plop here
and a plip-plop there -
Here a plip!
There a plop!
Everywhere a plip-plop!
Siggy Viking had a...'

**'SIGGY! WHAT ON EARTH ARE YOU
DOING?'** Mrs Ellis stood on the pavement gazing
up at the front of the hotel in disbelief. There was
bright green paint everywhere.

Sigurd had spilled great green puddles all over the entrance. Then he had walked in the puddles and left bright green bootprints up and down the porch. There were bright green handprints all over the walls. Most of Sigurd's helmet was bright green, and so were his clothes. He grinned down at Mrs Ellis.

'I go painting,' he said proudly. 'With a plip-plop here and a...'

'But you've painted all the windows!' yelled Mrs Ellis, almost beside herself.

'Mr Ellis said paint the doors and the railings and the windows,' nodded Sigurd.

'BUT YOU'VE PAINTED ALL THE GLASS!' screamed Mrs Ellis. 'All our windows are bright green! Nobody can see out anymore - Mr and Mrs Ramsbottom think it's still night-time and won't come down for breakfast!'

On the other side of the road Mr Crump opened his front door to see what all the fuss was about and stepped straight on to an upturned lid of bright green paint. He boggled at the shining green hotel opposite, shook his foot angrily and sent the paint-lid skimming back along his hall, where it left a nice green skid trail the entire length of the carpet. Mrs Ellis took one look at his angry face, ran inside, bolted the door and rushed upstairs to the bedroom. Another very severe case of Vikingitis had just taken hold.

3

Let's all be Friends!

It was an impossible task. The green paint stuck to the glass like glue and no matter what the Ellises tried they could not get the paint off. Eventually Mr Ellis had to call out some decorators. The glass had to be removed from the window frames and replaced. The decorators had to re-do all the painting properly and then they presented Mr Ellis with a big bill for the work. He was not very pleased, although he did blame himself for what had happened .

'I had forgotten just how stupid Sigurd can be,' he muttered.

'You did tell him to paint the windows,' Zoe pointed out. 'So he did.'

'Thank you Zoe, for that helpful comment,' Mr Ellis replied icily.

Mrs Ellis folded her arms. 'We are going to have to do something, Keith. We can't have Sigurd ruining everything we've worked so hard for.'

'I know. If only we could think of a way to get him out of the hotel most of the time. At least he wouldn't be under our feet then. Tim and Zoe go to school, which gets them out of the way. It's a shame Sigurd is too old for school.' His voice trailed away and a faint wisp of a smile flickered across his face. 'We can't get him into school, can we?'

'He is a bit big for Playgroup, which is where he should be,' Mrs Ellis admitted. 'He'd love Playgroup - all that sand and water...'

'And paint,' added Mr Ellis. 'They always do lots of painting.'

'The trouble is, I think the school would notice. Imagine Siggy arriving for the day. He'd be standing there in his school uniform, with his bent helmet rammed on his head and Nosepicker by his side...' Penny Ellis began to laugh. 'No, I'm afraid he's too big for school.'

'He can come to school with me,' said Tim, poking his head round the door. 'The other children would think it was brill.'

'Brill? Who taught you to speak like that?' asked Mr Ellis.

'Speak like what?' asked Tim. 'Anyway, Siggy can come in with me tomorrow. Mr Rumble will like that.'

'I doubt it,' murmured Mrs Ellis. 'I don't think it's a good idea, Tim.'

'Oh go on,' pleaded Tim. 'Everyone else brings things in. James brought in his rabbit last week, and Rachel Wagstaff had an eskimo doll made out of whalebone and sealskin.'

'Yes, but a real person is rather different,' said Mrs Ellis, still shaking her head.

'A real person is even better,' pronounced Tim. 'People can see rabbits any day they want and anyway it did a poo on James' desk. And the doll was boring and the sealskin stank. A real Viking would be brilliant. Siggy can tell the whole class about what it was like in Viking times, and Mr Rumble will like it 'cos he always does when people bring things in 'cos he doesn't have to do so much teaching, and Siggy won't do poos like the rabbit and he doesn't stink either - well, not much anyway.'

Tim's parents listened to this long speech with growing astonishment. 'Good grief,' said his father. 'I didn't know you had so many words inside you, Tim.'

'I've got billions of words inside me,' Tim explained. 'But most of the time I think them rather than say them. Sometimes when I say things it comes out all wrong, only it didn't just then. The words all came out right.'

Mr Ellis laughed. 'They certainly did.'

'So can Siggy come into school with me then?'

Mrs Ellis nodded. 'We'll give it a try, Tim. But he had better behave himself. Go and tell him. He's upstairs. Mrs Tibblethwaite locked him in their room to make sure he didn't cause any more damage.' Tim vanished in a flash and a moment later the Ellises heard the sound of his feet charging up the stairs.

'Strange how one pair of feet can sound like a whole herd of dinosaurs,' mused Mrs Ellis. 'I hope we've made the right decision, Keith.'

'Put it this way,' said Mr Ellis. 'Tomorrow Siggy will be out of our hair almost the whole day. I can't think of anything better.'

Tim and Zoe both felt extremely proud the next day. They walked into school on either side of Siggy, holding his hands. The children and teachers all knew about Sigurd of course. Many of them had seen him when he went shopping in Flotby with the Ellises, but it was quite different to have him in their school. A real Viking in their school!

Most of the boys wanted Sigurd to get out Nosepicker and do some swordfighting but Zoe was very sensible and managed to prevent a major disaster in the playground. 'We'll show them later, Sigurd,' she said. Then there was a bit of a scuffle because they all wanted to try on his helmet. And finally Zoe and Tim had a quarrel over whose class Sigurd would go to first, and Tim won, because it had been his idea.

At Assembly Mrs Crock, the head teacher, introduced Sigurd to the whole school. Mrs Crock was a slim, small lady, with neat grey hair fixed in a bun. She always stood on a little box to talk to the children, but even so, she was still shorter than Sigurd.

The Viking stood next to her with his black hair exploding from beneath his battered helmet, and a fierce smile on his face.

'Children,' began Mrs Crock. 'We are delighted to have Sigurd the Viking with us this week. He will be telling you what it was like to be a Viking and everything about Viking life. Sigurd is an important visitor, so please look after him well. Sigurd, would you like to say something?'

Sigurd stepped forward and beamed at everyone in the hall. 'I Sigurd. I come from Hedeby, Denmark. How do I do and the same to you.' He pointed round the big room. 'This cruel. I like cruel.' Mrs Crock nudged him gently.

'School,' she hissed.

'Yes - scrool!' said Sigurd cheerfully. 'Scrool good place. You learn much things. I teach you Viking things. I make you good Vikings. Now I say cheerio and shake your hands and goodbye Mrs Crocodile.' Sigurd turned to the head teacher, threw his arms round her, gave her an enormous, loud kiss on each cheek and then rubbed his nose against hers. 'There!'

Mrs Crock almost fell from her wooden box. She stood there rocking back on her feet, quite speechless, while Sigurd grinned at everyone. 'That old Viking custom,' he said. 'You watch. I show you again,' and before Mrs Crock could escape she found herself captured in the Viking's hairy arms once again. 'Now everyone try,' cried Sigurd. 'Everybody stand up. You go to person next to you...'

Nobody moved. The teachers stared back at him, aghast, as their head teacher fainted, and slowly sank to the floor. The children watched and hoped they didn't really have to do all this hugging and kissing and nose-rubbing, but Sigurd was adamant. He whipped out Nosepicker and brandished it furiously above his head.

'Everybody stand up!' he ordered. 'Now you put arms round necks, hugsy-wugsy, and kiss on chops, slopsy-wopsy, then rub noses, grotty-snotty.'

The hall was an extraordinary sight. Two hundred and thirty children began shouting and grappling with each other. Eight teachers turned red with embarrassment and began hugging one another.

'You be very careful, Mr Rumble,' warned Mrs Blatt. 'My husband is a policeman.'

'You be careful,' he answered coldly, 'or I shall have to report you to him.'

From the children came a great moan of disgust. Even Tim and Zoe were unsure of this Viking custom.

'Urgh! You kissed me Zoe!'

'Well I tried not to. Do you think I wanted to kiss you? You should have kept your face out of the way. I shall probably get the plague now.'

'Yuk! Get your nose off me!' shouted Rachel Wagstaff to some poor five year old, who immediately burst into tears.

Sigurd was very pleased, and he stood there grinning at everyone. He didn't seem to notice that several fights had now broken out between the children, and between the teachers too. Those that weren't fighting or arguing were crying. They didn't like this Viking custom at all.

'Now we all good friends!' Sigurd declared, ignoring the fact that the hall was a wriggling mass of squealing bodies, all trying to escape. He bent down, picked up the unconscious Mrs Crock and threw her over one shoulder. He knew just how to bring her round.

Sigurd marched off down the corridor with the head teacher dangling over his shoulder. He poked his head round every door and at last found a wash-room. He propped up Mrs Crock on the tiled floor, filled a nearby mop bucket with cold water and poured the entire contents over the hapless head.

Mrs Crock jerked, gulped, coughed, spluttered and opened her eyes. Her hair straggled down her face and shoulders and her make-up trickled down her cheeks, making long, blue-black smudges. She sat there in an enormous pool of water and stared up at the Viking who was busily refilling his bucket.

'Noooooo! Keep away from me!' she shouted. She leapt to her feet and was off down the corridor at top squelching speed.

'Mrs Crocodile all right now,' Sigurd said to himself as he watched her vanish with great satisfaction. He had been in school for less than half an hour, and already he had reduced the place to a shambles.

4

All at Sea

Sigurd and Tim and Zoe stood in the head teacher's office looking across at Mrs Crock. 'I think we got off to a bad start,' said the head teacher. One of the cooks from the school kitchen had kindly lent the head teacher a cook's uniform, so that she had something dry to wear. Mrs Crock's hair was still rather bedraggled, and she had poked it up underneath a cook's cap. Tim was very surprised to see Mrs Crock in a blue uniform.

'Are you going to do the cooking today, Mrs Crock?' Zoe, who knew exactly why Mrs Crock was dressed like a cook, nudged her brother, but it was too late. Mrs Crock fixed him with a steely glare.

'No, Tim, I am not going to do the cooking today. I am wearing this uniform because... because I wet my dress earlier and I had to change.'

Tim's eyes almost popped out of his head. 'You wet yourself!' he whispered in awe. Mrs Crock went very red.

'Of course I didn't! Don't be so stupid! I meant that my dress became wet. In fact it was soaked, by your Viking friend here.' Now the head teacher glared at Sigurd, and he shrugged.

'I try to help,' he explained.

Mrs Crock sighed. 'I know. I understand that it was a mistake. However, if you are going to visit the classrooms today then I must ask you to make sure that you do not make the children, or the teachers, do anything silly: like all that ridiculous kissing and hugging.'

'Viking custom,' growled Sigurd.

'Yes, I know it's a Viking custom. But we are not Vikings. We are civilised human beings.'

Sigurd frowned. 'Scoose me,' he said. 'What is silly-fly human bean?'

'Oh never mind.' Poor Mrs Crock felt totally exhausted, and it was only a quarter to ten. 'Tim, take Sigurd to your class, and please, please make sure he doesn't do anything stupid.'

'I not stupid,' Sigurd protested.

'Of course you're not,' smiled Mrs Crock, showing them the door and closing it behind them.

'You're just a complete and utter nutcase,' she muttered to herself before collapsing into a chair. Wearily she pulled open a little drawer in her desk and got out a small, silver hip-flask. It was astonishing how many people in Flotby had hip-flasks. Sales were on the increase now that Sigurd was back in town.

Sigurd squeezed himself into the chair next to Tim, just managing to get his knees under the table. Tim grinned at his classmates, and they stared back at the great big hairy Viking sitting in their classroom. Mr Rumble smiled.

'We are very lucky this morning, children. Tim's friend Sigurd is going to tell us about Viking times. I shall sit down in this quiet corner. Sigurd - why don't you come to the front of the class?'

The Viking beamed with pleasure and got up. Unfortunately his knees were still jammed under the table which overbalanced and crashed to the floor. Rachel Wagstaff sniggered.

'He's very clumsy for a Viking,' she murmured. 'I bet he's not a real Viking. He's just pretend.'

'He is real!' hissed Tim, as he put the table back on its legs. 'And you can shut up, Rachel.'

Rachel's hand shot into the air and waved about madly. 'Mr Rumble, Tim told me to shut up!'

'Good idea,' thought Mr Rumble, but he smiled and said: 'Over to you, Sigurd. What are you going to tell us about?'

Sigurd took off his helmet, scratched his head, put his helmet back on and stared at his feet. 'I Viking!' he announced.

'Yes, we know that,' sighed Mr Rumble.

'I Sigurd, from Hedeby, Denmark.'

'Yes. We know that too.'

'I fierce warrior.' Sigurd pulled his fiercest face and Mandy Perkins screamed. Mandy Perkins was always screaming about something.

'He's only pretending,' Tim pointed out with a groan.

'It's all right, Mandy, Sigurd is acting,' explained Mr Rumble. He turned to the Viking. 'Tell us about life in Hedeby, Sigurd.'

'Hedeby - my town. Lots of Vikings: some big like me, some small like baby, some young like Tim, some old like Crumble...'

'Rumble!' snapped Mr Rumble. 'And I'm not that old either, if you don't mind. What did you eat?'

Sigurd closed his eyes and licked his lips. 'Sometimes we have big feet,' he said. 'Very big feet to praise Thor, God of Thunder.'

'He means feast,' whispered Tim to the rest of the class, who were beginning to giggle.

'We eat chickens and pigs and sheets and coats.'

'Sheep and goats,' muttered Tim.

'I don't think people should eat meat,' said Rachel. 'I'm a vegetarian.' Sigurd scowled, leant over Rachel's table and put one hand on Nosepicker.

'Vikings kill vegetables,' he hissed.

'Oh!' squeaked Rachel, and she didn't say anything else for a long time.

After that things went quite well for a while. The children became engrossed in what Sigurd told them and they began asking questions. Tim sat back proudly and listened to his tenth-century friend and Mr Rumble dozed quietly in the corner. It was when Terry Reeves started asking about Viking longships that things began to go wrong - again. Terry wanted to know how everyone knew when to row.

'I went in a rowing boat with my dad once,' he said. 'I had two oars and he had two oars but we couldn't put them in the water at the same time. We just went round and round until he bashed one of my oars with his oar and they both broke and we got told off and had to be rescued.'

Sigurd nodded; this was a problem he knew well. He was hopeless at rowing himself but he would never admit it. In fact, he pretended he was pretty good at it. 'I show you how we row,' he declared. 'First we put tables on sides like this.' He made two rows of tables down the classroom, with their legs pointing inwards. 'Now you put cheese down middle.'

'Cheese?' repeated Terry. 'I haven't got any cheese.'

'I've got some cheese in my sandwich,' James said. 'But that's for my lunch.'

'I think he might mean chairs,' Tim suggested.

'Cheese!' grinned Sigurd, picking up one chair after another, and putting them in rows of four between the tables. 'Now we get oars.'

Tim stared at the tables and chairs. 'Siggy's made a longship!' he cried. 'Look, the tables are the sides of the boat and the chairs are the benches that the rowers sit on. Brill - I'll get some oars! James - you come with me, and Terry.' The three boys dashed out of the classroom, while Mr Rumble snored away in the corner, dreaming about being a Viking.

A few moments later Tim and the others came racing back. They had raided the caretaker's cupboard and taken a whole assortment of long-handled brooms, mops, window-openers and anything that was long, thin and vaguely oar-like.

'Now you take oars!' cried Siggy. The children settled into their seats and seized their oars. 'We go Hedeby! Oars forward!'

Fourteen assorted mops, brooms and window-openers waved in the air. Several flowerpots were knocked from the windowsill on the port side, while on the starboard bow a rack of newly-filled paint-pots crashed to the floor and began making a multicoloured ocean for the longship to sail across.

Sigurd had never seen such hopeless rowing. He leapt on to Mr Rumble's desk and pulled Nosepicker from its tatty scabbard. 'You keep time with me!' he roared, beating out a rowing rhythm on Mr Rumble's desk with Nosepicker's heavy blade. 'In! Out! In! Out!' Large chips of wood splintered off the desk and spun through the air.

The longship was beginning to sink. The rowers were all quarrelling because they kept hitting each other with their brooms and mops. Mandy Perkins started screaming. Sally threw a flowerpot at Adam because she thought he'd flicked her with paint and Terry pushed Tim overboard.

Sigurd jumped up and down so much that he managed to jam the horns of his helmet into one of the overhead light fittings and rip it from the ceiling. He couldn't quite keep his balance with a large fluorescent light fitting waving about on his helmet and after a few seconds, he went tumbling down into Mr Rumble's lap.

'Eh? Eh? EH!' cried Mr Rumble, scrambling
out from beneath Sigurd. He gazed round his
classroom. Children were crawling through a
mixed-up sea of paint, mud and flowers and
prodding each other with mops and brooms.
Plaster trickled down from the ceiling where
Sigurd had ripped out the light, and now the
Viking was on his feet and striding round the
classroom, still with a light tube stuck on his
helmet and shouting 'In! Out! In! Out!'

Mr Rumble joined in. 'Out! Out! Out!' he
bellowed, seizing a window-pole and poking
Sigurd. 'Get out of my classroom at once! You're
not a Viking - you're a disaster!' And with one final,
vicious prod he sent Sigurd scampering up the
corridor.

It was now almost twelve o'clock and Sigurd had
reduced the school to a shambles a second time.

5

A Viking all Alone

At lunch time, Mrs Crock took Sigurd home. She had taken one look at Mr Rumble's shipwrecked classroom and decided it was the best thing to do. Zoe and Tim went with her to keep an eye on Sigurd.

Mr and Mrs Ellis were not surprised to see Sigurd being frog-marched up the hotel steps by Mrs Crock, but they were rather bemused by the cook's uniform the head teacher was wearing. Zoe noticed both her parents staring.

'It's a long story,' she began.

'It's a wet story,' Tim added.

Mrs Crock only stopped long enough to make a brief announcement. 'If this Viking comes anywhere near my school ever again I shall kill him,' she said bluntly. 'I shall probably strangle him with my bare hands. I might even slice him up on my paper-trimmer and put the bits in a thousand different files in my filing cabinet.'

'Things didn't work out, then?' offered Mr Ellis.

'That, Mr Ellis, is an understatement.' Mrs Crock turned on her heels and strode back to the car. The door slammed, the engine revved and with a great deal of wheelspin Mrs Crock vanished.

'Wow! Can she drive!' breathed Tim.

There was a long, cold, silent pause, while everyone stood on the hotel steps. Sigurd tried a helpful smile, and his dark eyes shot from one Ellis to another. Even Tim could sense that there was trouble ahead - big trouble. He felt for his sister's hand and together they slipped quietly into the hotel. They hid behind the front door and listened, desperate to know what was going to happen.

Mr and Mrs Ellis stood across the hotel doorway, blocking the entrance. 'You can't come in,' said Mr Ellis. 'I'm sorry Sigurd, but we're not having you back here. Every time you turn up there is trouble. We cannot afford to keep paying for the mistakes you make and we are not prepared to let you live in our hotel any longer. You've got to go. Mrs Tibblethwaite can stay here until she finds somewhere more suitable. In the meantime you will just have to manage for yourself.'

Tim and Zoe came racing out from behind the front door. 'Dad! Mum! You can't throw him out!'

'Oh yes we can,' said Mrs Ellis. 'It might seem cruel to you, but Sigurd has to go. He has cost us hundreds, probably thousands of pounds. He has driven everyone mad. Your father and I cannot cope any longer. We have enough worries trying to run this hotel, especially with business so bad at present.'

'But throwing him out!' Zoe cried. 'It's not right. He'll be homeless.'

'I've thought of that,' said Mr Ellis. 'He can stay in the greenhouse until Mrs Tibblethwaite finds somewhere better for him.'

'The greenhouse? But Dad, half the glass is broken.'

'I know. Sigurd was the one who broke it, so that's his problem. Come on, everyone inside, the Ramsbottoms are waiting for their lunch.' Mr Ellis pushed his children into the hotel with Mrs Ellis following hard on their heels. She turned on the doorstep and eyed Sigurd sternly.

'You've made all these problems, Siggy,' she said. 'Just for once, you sort them out.'

She stepped inside and shut the door, leaning back against it, her face white and drawn. She was certain that this was the hardest thing she had ever done in her life; but it had to be done. Somehow Sigurd had to understand his responsibilities to other people.

Sigurd stood on the hotel porch, gazing at the closed door. All his friends, all the people he most loved were on the other side of that door, shut away from him. He backed slowly down the hotel steps, his eyes fixed on the front of The Viking Hotel, but the door didn't open. Then he turned and walked away.

Tim and Zoe sat on Zoe's bed with their backs

to the wall and their knees hunched up against their chests. 'The thing is,' said Zoe, 'Siggy could be out there anywhere. Anything might have happened to him by now.'

'He could have been kidnapped,' suggested Tim.

'Yeah...,' said Zoe, although she couldn't imagine why anyone in their right mind would want to kidnap a smelly, dirty Viking warrior like Sigurd.

'He might have had all his blood sucked out by Dracula,' Tim continued. Zoe thought that this was also rather unlikely.

'Or chewed to bits by a werewolf, or snatched from the planet by aliens with three heads and ten legs....'

'Tim!'

Tim frowned to himself and counted carefully on his fingers before turning to his sister. 'Zoe, if you have ten legs does that mean you must have five bottoms?'

'TIM! What are we going to do about Siggy?'

'It's Dad's fault,' muttered Tim through his teeth.

'And Mum's,' Zoe added. 'They should be arrested and taken to court and charged with um....' Zoe couldn't quite decide what her parents ought to be charged with.

'Cruelty to Vikings,' suggested Tim.

'Yeah, something like that.' There was a short silence during which Tim gave up trying to think for himself.

'Maybe we could smuggle him back into the hotel,' Zoe murmured.

'Smuggle him back in? Brilliant idea! We could hide him in my room!'

'I don't think that would work Tim. The best place for him would be one of the empty guest rooms.'

'You can be quite clever sometimes, for a girl.'

Zoe glanced up at her brother's smiling face. 'And you can be quite stupid,' she replied. 'Most of the time.' Tim's smile vanished.

'That's not very nice,' he grumbled. She grinned and grabbed hold of his hand.

'Come on. Let's see if we can find Siggy. He'll probably be down on the beach somewhere. He always goes and stares at the sea when he's upset about something.'

'How do you know?' asked Tim, who had never noticed anything of the sort.

'Because I'm a girl and I'm clever.'

Tim had no answer to this. It was a real pain being two years younger than his sister. It meant that Zoe was always two years older. She was always ahead of him. He would never, ever be able to catch her up. Life was very unfair.

Zoe was right, too. Sigurd was down on the beach, standing at the water's edge and staring out at the flat, grey shimmering sea, while little waves rolled up to his feet and frothed over them. The children went and stood quietly at his side.

'Siggy?' Zoe held his big hand.

'Mmmmm?'

'What are you thinking?'

'I think Sigurd stupid,' growled the Viking. 'He biggest stupid in whole world.'

'No you're not!' cried Tim.

'More stupid than donkey; more stupid than dog; even more stupid than eeny-weeny-teeny-titchy-witchy-snitchy mouse.'

'No you're not!' Tim repeated. Sigurd gave a big gloomy sigh and threw a stone into the sea.

'I more stupid than carrot,' he announced sadly.

Zoe felt that the conversation was rapidly slipping into a list of animals and vegetables. Sigurd could probably keep up this display of self-pity for hours. 'Listen, Tim and I have got an idea. We could smuggle you back into the hotel.'

'Scoose me, what is smuggle?'

'We sneak you into the hotel when no one's looking, and you can hide in one of the spare rooms.'

Sigurd picked up another stone and hurled it as far as he could. The stone seemed to curve through the air for ages before at last it dived down into the distant sea. A burst of foam exploded into the air, marking where the stone hit the surface, before it vanished from sight. Sigurd turned to Zoe and shook his head.

'No,' he said firmly. 'I no go smuggling and sneaking. Mr, Mrs Ellis - they very angry with Sigurd. They right. I bad man.'

'You're not bad!' protested Zoe. 'You're just, sort of, different.'

'I make mess,' Sigurd went on. 'I break things, make people cross. I no good in hotel. I good one thing only - make trouble. Trouble easy-peasy for me. People say - Sigurd, what you do? I say I do trouble. I do good trouble. You want big trouble, small trouble, or piddle-size trouble?'

'Sigurd,' pleaded Zoe. 'Don't go on like that. Please come back to the hotel.'

But the Viking pulled his big hand away from hers. 'Go home Tim. Go home Zoe. I find place to sleep. Maybe I go to bluehouse like Mr Ellis say.'

'Greenhouse,' said Tim. 'Not bluehouse.'

Sigurd shrugged. 'Greenhouse, bluehouse - it good place for man like carrot. You clever - hotel your house. Now I stay here alone. Want to think.'

Tim and Zoe trudged back across the wet sand without him. 'He's not really as stupid as a carrot, is he?' asked Tim.

'Of course he isn't. He's just feeling a bit sorry for himself.'

'And he isn't trouble either, is he?'

Zoe thought for a few moments before answering. 'Well, he is a bit,' she said. 'Really.' She walked several steps and then spoke again. 'I think that's why I like him so much.'

6

With a Mud-pat Here, and a Cow-pat There...

Tim and Zoe pleaded with their parents all evening, but it was no use. Even Mrs Tibblethwaite thought that Mr and Mrs Ellis had done the right thing. 'I would have thrown him out long ago,' she said.

'How can you say that?' shouted Zoe. 'You're married to him. You're supposed to love him!'

'Just because you love someone Zoe, it doesn't mean that you have to put up with everything they do. I do love Siggy, but most of the time he's like an enormous child. He has to learn how to behave.'

'Why?' asked Tim.

'Because that is what all people have to do, even tenth-century Vikings.'

'Huh!' Tim didn't think much of this at all. Zoe felt the same way as her brother, but she tried to put her feelings into proper words.

'People like Siggy because he's different,' she said. 'They like him because he doesn't behave the way the rest of us have to. That's what makes him such fun.'

Mrs Ellis managed a faint smile. 'I'm sure you're right Zoe, but you have to admit that it is difficult for us. It's all right for other people to laugh at Siggy's stupid mistakes; they don't have to pick up the pieces and pay for the damage, or live with him day-by-day. We do.'

'You won't let him back in then?' Tim asked.

'No,' said Mr Ellis. 'Sorry.'

'Then I shall never speak to you again and I'm going on strike.'

'But you don't do anything,' Mr Ellis pointed out.

'A hunger strike,' Tim said, glaring at his parents. 'I shan't eat anything until you let Siggy back into the hotel.' Hah! They'd soon change their minds now!

'Fine,' said Mrs Ellis. 'That should save us some money on food bills at any rate.'

'You'll let me starve?' cried Tim.

Mr Ellis shook his head. 'Of course not, Tim. We wouldn't let you starve. We'll let you eat anytime. You're starving yourself.' Tim clenched his fists. This was too much. He'd been out-argued again.

He leapt to his feet and stamped out of the room. Zoe watched him go.

'Now look what you've done!' she cried, and ran from the room in tears.

Mr and Mrs Ellis glanced across at Mrs Tibblethwaite. 'Oh dear,' said Mrs Ellis. 'It is hard.'

'Hard for everyone,' agreed Mrs T. 'But don't worry. I'm sure things will turn out all right in the end. Tim won't go for long without eating.'

'Oh I know that,' said Mrs Ellis. 'It's Zoe I'm worried about.'

Mrs Tibblethwaite reached forward and patted Mrs Ellis on the hand. 'Zoe is a clever girl, and sensitive too. I'm sure she understands really, and that's why it upsets her so much. Siggy will be all right. Goodness, he must have spent hundreds of nights outside, sleeping under the stars when he was a proper Viking in proper Viking times. I wouldn't worry about him at all. Goodnight!'

Tim stuck to his guns. He refused supper and he turned down a drink and a biscuit before bedtime. By the time he crawled into bed he was starving. His stomach was aching for food and he cursed himself for saying that he was on hunger-strike. He tossed and turned for hours and was just drifting off to sleep when he heard the bedroom door open. Zoe quickly slipped into the room and shut the door. She tiptoed across to the bed.

'Are you awake?'

'Of course I'm awake. My stomach is making very loud empty noises. I can't sleep.'

'I've brought you some food,' Zoe whispered, and she pulled two chunky sandwiches from inside her dressing-gown. 'That one's got a bit of fluff on it I'm afraid. I had to hide them under here.'

'That's okay,' said Tim, stuffing it into his mouth.
'I like fluff sandwiches. Thanks. I was starving.'

'I knew you would be. Anyway, it was very
brave of you to go on hunger strike.'

'Yeah? Yeah! It was. I could have died.'

'Tim - you've only been without food for
about ten hours,' laughed Zoe.

'Ten hours? It feels more like ten months.'

Zoe sat down on the edge of Tim's bed. 'I'll try and get something for you tomorrow at breakfast. Mr Travis always leaves his toast and...' Zoe stopped in mid-sentence, frowned, and went across to the window. She pulled back the curtains a little way and peered into the darkness. 'Did you hear something?' she asked her brother.

'No? Did you?' Tim slipped out of bed and joined Zoe at the window. Now they could both hear odd sounds from outside. Bumping, banging and dragging noises drifted up from the back garden of the hotel.

'Is that someone humming?' asked Tim.

'I don't know,' Zoe answered, 'but I think I just saw a pig.'

'A pig! Don't be daft!'

'Well it looked like a pig,' Zoe insisted.

'It could have been a werewolf,' whispered her brother, his eyes growing bigger and bigger. 'Or a ghost.'

'It was a pig,' repeated Zoe.

'Maybe it was a ghost-pig,' Tim went on. 'The Ghastly Ghost-Pig of Flotby. Or maybe even a were-pig-wolf-ghost-thingy...'

'A were-ghost-pig-wolf-whotsit?'

'Yeah - with fangs that shine in the dark and X-ray eyes and stuff...'

Zoe pulled the curtains back into place and summoned up her courage. 'Well, whatever it is, there's something going on out there. I'm going downstairs to see what it is.'

'And I'm coming with you,' said Tim, who suddenly felt that he didn't want to be left alone. He grabbed his torch.

The two children crept silently down the back stairs and tiptoed out through the hotel kitchen. Zoe quietly unlocked the back door. The noises were much louder now - grunts and squeaks and bangs and thuds. Zoe felt for Tim's hand. 'Are you scared?' she whispered.

'No,' lied Tim. 'Are you?'

'Yes, a bit.'

'Then I am too,' Tim decided. They pressed forward across the path and on to the dark lawn, moving slowly towards the source of all the noise. They had just reached the nearest corner of the greenhouse when a huge, dark figure loomed right in front of them, giving the children the most enormous fright.

'Aargh!' screamed Tim, dropping his torch and running like mad across the lawn. 'It's the were-ghost!'

'Aaargh!' screeched Zoe, racing off in the other direction. 'It's a pig-wolf!'

'Aaaargh!' bellowed Sigurd, dropping a large pile of sticks, and drawing Nosepicker. 'It's rubbers! You bad peoples - come to rub hotel. I kill rubbers!'

Tim stopped running and looked back at the
Viking. 'I'm not a rubber, I mean robber,' he said
crossly. 'I'm Tim.'

Sigurd stopped poking the night air with
Nosepicker and calmed down. 'You give me fright,'
he told Tim and Zoe.

'You gave us a fright!' said Zoe. 'But I'm glad you're all right, Siggy. What are you doing out here?'

Sigurd slipped Nosepicker back into its scabbard. His white teeth flashed a moonlit grin. 'I show you. I stand on beach and think very hard. Tide coming in. Water come up to my knees. I still thinking what to do. Water come to tummy. I still think. Water come to neck. Think I drown so get out of sea and walk down road. Then I have pig idea.'

'Big idea,' corrected Zoe.

'No,' said Sigurd. 'Pig idea. Look.'

Sigurd led the children over to the far corner of the hotel garden. Siggy had made a kind of pen. He had banged wooden posts into the ground and woven branches in between the posts. He had covered the branches with some kind of muddy mixture that was still drying. And on the other side of the pen were three extremely large pigs. They gazed sleepily at Tim and Zoe. One gave a quiet "oink".

'You did all this?' murmured Zoe admiringly. 'It's called wattle and daub, isn't it? I didn't know you could make fences, Siggy.'

'Vikings always make fences like this. Put in post, bang-bang. Put in branches. Mix up mud and straw and cow-stuff...'

'Cow-stuff?' Tim repeated, not sure if he wanted to hear about how to make a wattle and daub fence.

183

'They mixed in cow-pats as well,' explained Zoe.

'Urgh, that's revolting!' cried Tim. Sigurd shook his head.

'I no find cows. No cow-stuff, but good fence anyway.'

'Where did the pigs come from?' asked Zoe.

'I find them.'

'You found three pigs?'

It was very dark, so Tim and Zoe couldn't see how red Sigurd had gone. He went back to the greenhouse to collect the pile of wood he had dropped. 'Actually, I find four pigs, walking down road, but one run away, trit-trot. She big pig. Very big pig. She big bad pig. You see pig?'

'No, we no see pig - I mean we didn't see a pig anywhere,' replied Zoe.

'Never mind. Now I build house for Sigurd,' said the Viking, and he began banging in a row of tall posts. 'Hotel too smart for Viking. I make Viking house in garden. Take long time. You go bed. I see you in...'

'Eeeeeek!'

'Aaaargh!'

Startled screams from the hotel interrupted Sigurd in mid-sentence. A bedroom window flew open and the children watched, astonished, as their parents clambered out at top speed, as if the hotel was on fire.

Mrs Ellis managed to
grab hold of the thick ivy
running up one side of
the window frame, but
Mr Ellis was left dangling
from the window-ledge
by his fingertips. A few
seconds later there was
a loud and angry grunt
and a huge sow shoved
her trotters up on the
window-sill and peered
out, snorting and sniffing
like a flesh-eating ogre.
'Help! Help!' cried Mr
Ellis. 'Someone save us!
There's a giant pig in
our bedroom!'

7

Three Cheers for Sigurd!

Sigurd leapt to the rescue. He grabbed a ladder from behind the greenhouse and dashed across to the hotel. Penny Ellis had managed to clamber down the ivy, but her husband was still hanging by his fingernails. In a flash Siggy had raced up the ladder and plucked Mr Ellis from the window-ledge. He flung him over his shoulder and quickly backed down the ladder, while the murderous pig began shredding the Ellis's best velvet curtains with its vicious teeth.

'Sigurd, you saved my life,' panted Mr Ellis. 'I'm very grateful to you, but what do we do now? The pig's already eaten one of the hall rugs, several pot plants and that lovely painting we had of Flotby harbour.'

'Where did the pig come from anyway?' asked Mrs Ellis. 'Is this anything to do with you, Sigurd?'

'It wasn't his fault,' Tim blurted out. 'Siggy found them, on the road.'

'Them?' repeated Mr Ellis. 'Please don't tell me there are some more? And how can you find a pig on the road? That's ridiculous.'

Zoe pulled her parents over to Sigurd's pig pen. Mr and Mrs Ellis stared at the three sleepy occupants. 'Siggy made this,' explained Zoe. 'Isn't he clever? It's a wattle and daub fence, and now he's making a little house too - look.'

'Don't change the subject, Zoe. Where did the pigs come from? You don't find pigs just walking down the road as if they were off to do their shopping,' snapped Mr Ellis.

Sigurd burst out laughing. 'Pig do shopping! Ha ha! Very good! Very funny! This little piggy go to market!'

'They're not little piggies at all, Sigurd. They're the biggest piggies I have ever seen. You stole them didn't you? You stole them from the farm up near the cliffs.'

Sigurd's smile vanished and he shook his head seriously. 'I no steal! I find on road. I walk up road. Pig walk down road. One, two, three, four pig. I say "hallo pig! You come walkies with me. I make you nice home." Pig follow me. I come here and make fence for pig but one run away. She very big, like dragon. It dark. I no see where she go. Maybe she hungry. Maybe she go hotel. Now she eat curtains.'

Zoe tugged anxiously at the Viking's sleeve. 'Siggy, I think Mrs Tibblethwaite is still in there,' she whispered. Mr Ellis gave a despairing cry.

'So are Mr Travis and the Ramsbottoms!'

'No fear, Sigurd here!' roared the Viking, and he whipped out Nosepicker. He brandished the great sword high above his head and struck his most heroic pose. 'Now I catch pig and save Viking Hotel, save everyone. Then you all cheer for me - "Hurrah for Sigurd! He brave! He clever! What we do without him?" So! I go, fight this pig-dragon.'

And with that brave speech Sigurd strode across to the hotel, leaving the Ellises standing on the lawn, speechless. They huddled close together, clinging to each other with their arms.

'It's the end,' muttered Mr Ellis. 'We may as well close down now. Nobody will ever want to come back to the hotel after this.'

Inside The Viking Hotel, Sigurd crept up the stairs, holding Nosepicker at the ready. His eyes glinted fiercely in the darkness. It hadn't occurred to him to switch on the lights. 'Are you there, piggy-wig? I come to get you. I make you into bacon. Siggy find piggy. Here-coochy-coochy-coochy!'

Sigurd reached the first bedroom door. He paused a moment, took hold of the handle, counted to three and then burst in. 'Aha! Raaaargh!' His fierce battle cry was greeted with a

startled scream as Mr and Mrs Ramsbottom leapt
from their sleep. Mr Ramsbottom fell out of
bed backwards and knocked himself out. Mrs
Ramsbottom screamed that her husband was dead
and fainted on the spot.

Sigurd searched under the bed. He opened the
wardrobe and poked Nosepicker into every corner,
filling the Ramsbottom's clothes with sword holes.
There was no pig hiding there. He grunted and
made for the next room.

'One, two, three - Aha! Raaaargh!'

Mr Travis was sitting up in bed watching television. He didn't even glance up at the Viking. 'Is that room service?' he said. 'It's about time you brought me that pot of tea. I've been waiting for... Good Heavens!' Mr Travis gave a muffled squeak as Sigurd lifted up one end of the bed and he found himself all rolled up in a bundle with the bed-covers.

The pig wasn't under the bed. Sigurd let it crash back down and went off to continue his search next door. By this time Mrs Ramsbottom had come to her senses, but unfortunately, her husband had not. Still thinking he was dead, she pulled the poor man out of the bedroom by his feet and screamed for help.

Meantime Sigurd had reached the bathroom. He was about to throw open the door when it burst open itself, sending him crashing back against the wall. Out of the bathroom ran a pig that was almost as big as two tigers tied together, and three times as dangerous.

Her head was the size of a dustbin - a dustbin with fangs. Her body was as big as a car-crusher. She came out of the bathroom and stood on the landing. In her mouth were the remains of a lavatory brush. Somehow she had managed to get the shower-attachment wrapped round her head, a towel draped coyly over her enormous behind, and a toilet roll fixed to one rear trotter, where it now left a nice long trail of paper.

Another door opened further down the corridor, and a rather sleepy figure appeared. 'What's all the noise?' asked Mrs Tibblethwaite. 'What's going...' She froze with terror. The pig was glaring straight at her with hungry piggy-eyes. The sow opened and shut its jaws several times and took a couple of steps forward.

Mrs T. threw a frightened glance at her husband. 'Siggy?' she whispered. 'There is a very, very big pig looking at me and I'm scared. What do I do?' Before Sigurd could reply, the pig took three more menacing steps towards Mrs T. and pinned her against the wall, licking her chops noisily.

Sigurd gripped Nosepicker tightly and crept out from behind the bathroom door, inching towards the pig's fat rear. His face took on a fierce scowl and then, with a terrible war-cry, he leapt in the air. 'Ya-ha-raaaaargh!' He gave the sow's bulging behind an enormous prod with Nosepicker and the pig leapt into the air too, with a most peculiar, howling grunt.

'Snnnrrrghoowowowrrrgh!'

Again and again Sigurd poked the pig with his sword, driving the car-crusher down the stairs. As they passed the Ramsbottom's room Mrs Ramsbottom took one look at the pig and the roaring Viking and fainted again, right on top of her husband, making a nice neat heap.

A large roll of bedding staggered out from bedroom number two and fell to the floor, where it spent a long time wriggling and squeaking before

Mrs Tibblethwaite finally managed to get Mr Travis disentangled. Meanwhile Sigurd continued to drive the pig down the stairs, out into the garden and across to his newly-built pig-pen. He slammed the gate shut.

Everyone rushed to the fence and looked over at the new prisoner. 'Wow,' muttered Mr Ellis. 'That is some pig! You were brave Sigurd. I wouldn't have wanted to face an animal as big as that on my own.'

'Three cheers for Siggy!' cried Tim, and the Ellises all cheered, but it wasn't long before gloom and doom descended once again as several rather upset guests began to stumble outside.

Mr and Mrs Ellis calmed them down with cups of tea and quite a lot of brandy. Mrs Tibblethwaite got the Ramsbottoms safely back into bed. She seemed to have convinced Mrs Ramsbottom that it had all been a bad dream. 'I'll just have another sip of this,' twittered Mrs Ramsbottom, clutching Mrs T.'s silver hip-flask. 'It will help me sleep.'

Sigurd was even allowed to go back to his old room with his wife. 'Just for one night,' warned Mr Ellis. 'We shall decide what to do in the morning.'

At last the Ellises themselves were able to go to bed. Zoe and Tim fell asleep the moment their heads touched the pillow but neither of their parents could sleep much. They were too busy worrying about what would happen the next day.

8

The Viking Village

The very first thing Mr Ellis did when he got up the next morning was ring the local farm. He was on the telephone for a long time. Mrs Ellis knew that the farmer was a grumpy so-and-so, and wouldn't take kindly to Sigurd 'borrowing' his pigs. In fact she thought they would be lucky if Sigurd didn't end up in court.

When her husband eventually managed to get away from the telephone Mrs Ellis was surprised to find him smiling. 'Mr Garret's coming over this minute,' said Mr Ellis. 'You won't believe this but he's delighted we've got the pigs. Sigurd was telling the truth. The pigs broke out from the farm yesterday evening. Garret's been searching high and low all night. They're worth several thousand pounds you know, especially Big Betty.'

'Oh! Well that's a relief at any rate. The Ramsbottoms don't seem to remember anything. They're both complaining of headaches though - I can't imagine why. Mr Travis has gone out to the pen. He told me he wanted to see if that pig was really as big as he thought it was last night.'

As soon as breakfast was over Tim and Zoe went out to see the pigs. Now that it was broad daylight they could see just how massive Big Betty was. She seemed quite happy, and none the worse for being poked with Nosepicker. Sigurd's wattle and daub fence looked pretty good too. Mr Travis was admiring the house that Sigurd had started.

'I've not seen a proper wattle and daub house actually being built, you know,' he mused. 'It's quite fascinating. Just like a proper Viking town. Sigurd ought to make a whole village.'

Zoe glanced at Tim, but he was busy scratching Big Betty's back with a long stick. She left her brother with Mr Travis and walked slowly back to the house in search of her parents.

'Mum? Dad? I've had an idea that might help things.' Zoe sounded so hesitant that both her parents looked at her with interest.

'Really?' said Mrs Ellis. 'What sort of idea?'

Zoe repeated what Mr Travis had said out by the pig-pen. 'It made me think,' she said. 'Maybe Sigurd could make a whole village - well, a small village, five or six houses maybe. He could even live out there. He could keep pigs and goats and chickens, like in a real Viking village.'

Mr Ellis laughed. 'It's a nice idea, Zoe. It would probably keep Siggy happy, but how would it help us?'

'Mr Travis said he thought it was fascinating. People would come to the hotel to see a Viking village with a real Viking.'

'Oh I don't think so,' said Mrs Ellis. 'People wouldn't come here just because there was a Viking village in the back garden.'

'Schools would,' said Zoe.

'Go on,' murmured Mr Ellis, rubbing his chin hard.

'Groups of school children could come here. They could learn about Flotby in Viking times and be part of a real Viking village, with a real Viking, and do real Viking things. Schools would think it was absolutely brilliant, and while they're in Flotby they would have to stay at our hotel.'

Mr Ellis hugged his daughter so hard she almost stopped breathing. 'That is a fantastic idea Zoe! It's totally amazing! Oh, it's so simple! Penny - what do you think?'

'I can't see how it can fail,' said Mrs Ellis. 'It's a stupendous idea, Zoe. Well done!'

'What's a stupendous idea?' asked a large, burly man with a tweed hat perched on top of his head.

'Ah, Mr Garret,' smiled Zoe's father. 'My daughter has just come up with a rather clever plan for our hotel. Let's see what you think of it. I'll tell you on the way out to Sigurd's pig-pen.'

They found Sigurd already out there, hard at work. He was inside the pen, building up the walls of his little house, while Mrs T. rubbed down one of the pigs. Mr Garret was highly surprised (and delighted) to see how well his pigs had been fenced in and looked after.

'You've got a natural way with farm animals,' he told Sigurd gruffly.

'I like pigs,' said Siggy. 'I like sheets and coats too, and wife.' He grinned at Mrs Tibblethwaite. 'Like wife most of all.'

'That's all right then,' smiled Mrs T., and gave him a kiss. 'You daft dumpling.'

'You must have been pretty good to get four pigs all the way down the road and shut up here,' said Mr Garret.

'We did have a bit of trouble with Big Betty,' said Mrs Ellis. 'But I'm glad you've got your pigs back.'

'How can I thank you?' Mr Garret asked. 'They're worth an awful lot to me.'

'There's no need for any thanks.'

But Mr Garret wanted to do something for the Ellises. He had been desperate when he had discovered the loss of his pigs, and he was genuinely delighted to have them back. 'Tell you what,' he said, 'this idea of young Zoe's - your Viking's going to need a few bits and pieces. He'll need hens for a start. I haven't got any sheep, but I have got an old billy goat he can keep here, and when Big Betty has her next litter he can come up to the farm and choose a piglet.'

Sigurd listened to this with growing excitement. He rushed across to Mr Garret, wrapped the poor farmer in his arms, kissed him on both cheeks and then rubbed noses with him.

'Gerroff!' shouted Mr Garret, trying to push Sigurd away. 'You big hairy ox!'

'You good man!' cried the Viking. 'I pray to Thor and tell him you very good and go to Valhalla when you die.' Sigurd turned to Mr Ellis. 'You good man too!' he roared, and opened his arms wide. 'Come to Siggy!'

'Oh no,' muttered Mr Ellis, backing away. 'No Siggy, leave me alone. I don't want to be hugged. Siggy! Go away!' He turned tail and fled, with Sigurd in hot pursuit. The others watched with delight.

'I never knew Dad could run that fast,' said Tim. A startled scream came from the far side of the hotel. Mrs Ellis giggled.

'He can't,' she said.